CRACKERS IN THE SCRUB

Adventures and Stories about Florida's Cracker Cowboys

by

Miles H. Plowden, III

CRACKERS IN THE SCRUB
Adventures and Stories about Florida's Cracker Cowboys

iUniverse books may be ordered through booksellers or by contacting:

iUniverse
1663 Liberty Drive
Bloomington, IN 47403
www.iuniverse.com
844-349-9409

ISBN: 978-1-4401-2900-1 (sc)
ISBN: 978-1-4401-2902-5 (hc)

Print information available on the last page.

iUniverse rev. date: 09/19/2022

ACKNOWLEDGEMENT

I wish to thank **God** for giving me the inspiration to write this book and to thank a special list of people who read, typed, retyped and edited this work of mine. The special people are **Judy** and **Jim Enos**, they are retired school teachers from Winter Haven, Florida, **Lisa Enos Smith, Scot Smith**, both of who edited and re-edited the manuscript, my Granddaughter **Treva Ann (Plowden) Lopez**, who typed and re-typed the manuscript. I dare not leave my lovely little wife **Carolyn Plowden** out of this praise as she read the raw pages and I kept her red pencil busy. **Carolyn** is a wonderful "author's widow," as she put up with me spending countless hours of research and at the computer writing this manuscript.

A special thankyou to **Phyllis Gilbert**, my mentor, and her ability to keep me from giving up on this and other work she inspired me to accomplish.

Then **Lisa** and **Treva** produced the manuscript and made it ready to send electronically to the Publisher, **iUniverse Inc.**, Bloomington, Indiana, and now **God** bless them as they will compile this into a book ready for the reader and lover of **Florida Cracker Cowboys** and their history.

I did not use the electronic spell check on these pages for with the use of the vernacular of the Cracker Cowboys would do permanent and irreversible damage to the spell check system. Smoke would rise from the bowels of this computer word processing machine.

Thank you for buying and reading this book,

Miles H. Plowden, III

CONTENTS

FOREWORD

"Too few of us Floridians, whether native-born or newcomers, know much about the cowboy period in our state's history. Cattle raising was an important part of the economy in the 19th century, and with cattle, came cowboys.

The West is not the only part of the country with cowboy lore and adventures; Florida has its share of tales about rough, hard-working, and hard-riding cowmen. Fortunately, some writers of today have taken time to research the era and have enriched our lives by sharing with us stories of this little known time in Florida history."

Phyllis Gilbert

(Phyllis Gilbert is a Winter Haven, Polk County, Florida pioneer. She is a retired Winter Haven High School English Teacher. Phyllis is my mentor and has had everything to do with my writing these and other stories.)

Throughout the history of Florida, very little has been written about Florida cowboys and the taming of the peninsula. There are numerous stories in the history of the northern part of the state, the west coast, and the east coast. Though more has been written about the history in these areas of the Sunshine State, there is a great deal of history here in central Florida. Battles with Indians were fought throughout the entire state, and central Florida is no exception.

I chose to write about the central Florida area because I was born and raised here. I did days of research about that area and the people who took the land to settle. Those who were first found nothing that glittered such as gold or silver. Those who would find riches there soon moved on, leaving only trails hacked and hewn from a wilderness of palmetto and oak thicket scrub. Centuries old hammocks of oak and hickory trees with cabbage palms dotted about. Not a very fetching legacy these trails, but nevertheless, a legacy. The trails were later used to discover other resources not seen through eyes blinded by gold fever.

Swamps with their pestilence, such as alligators, snakes, mosquitoes, yellow flies, horse flies, deer flies, and other vermin had to be overcome or circumnavigated. Any person who stayed longer than a few days surely knew that the spots with small red dots in the center itched like crazy. We called them redbugs. They lasted only until the offending animal was inadvertently scratched off or just died and fell off the skin. Then, and only then, would relief come to the victim. It is safe to say that the times, territory and climate were not conducive to rapid development nor influencing settlers to move to this tropical wonderland.

The Indians were the first to come across the plains and form inhabited areas near lakes, rivers, or fertile areas where they could make their livelihood. The Indians of Florida consisted of only four main groups. The Tegesta occupied the southeast and west coasts along with the Calusa tribe. The Timucua was more in the northern area of the state from Georgia, Alabama, and areas to the south, meeting the territory of the Calusa and Tegesta. The Apalachee extended into Georgia and west of the Aucilla River in the panhandle. All the tribes were hunter-gatherers except the Apalachee who grew crops of corn, pumpkins, squash, and beans and cultivated native persimmons and plums.

The Indians drove the scrub cattle into their camps and used them for beef, hides, milk and primitive milk products. (Later on, the Indians catching cattle became a sore subject with many of the cracker cowboys.) They also caught, tamed, and broke to halter, bit and saddle the wild horses in Florida called the Marsh Tacky. This small but wiry animal was best suited for driving cattle from the scrub, along with the cur or mongrel dogs. All of these tools were available to the settler through the resourcefulness of the Indians.

Animal and hunter trails gave way to wagon ruts, and wagon ruts to clay roads and then to asphalt. With each improvement more people came. They came to settle down and to build towns and railroads. Soon the Spanish fortresses became items of merely historical interest. They were no longer needed to defend the population. Like the Indians' gardens and their agriculture, the fortresses served a purpose and sustained the lives of so many in Florida, from conquistadors to astronauts.

PREFACE

In the small, paper-bound book, *FLORIDA THE LAND OF ROMANCE* is written: "The cattle business brought comparative wealth to the southwest coast. The Cuban insurrection that started in 1868 created a demand for beef to feed the Spanish army that was supplied from Florida. Cowboys drove cattle from the upper St. Johns, the Kissimmee River valley, and the prairies around Lake Okeechobee to Punta Rassa at the mouth of the Caloosahatchee River. There the herds were loaded in pens on steamboats for the trip to Havana. Florida cowboys did not work like western cowboys. They used mongrels called catch-dogs to round up cattle. When a cowboy wanted to throw a steer, he thrust his right arm across its back, caught it by the nose and horn, and turned it upside down in the air as it bucked. Instead of a lasso, he carried a cow-dragger, a whip twenty feet long made of braided buckskin, whose snap or crack sounded like a gun. Although the name "cracker" was applied to Georgia and Florida country people long before there were Florida cowboys, it is supposed to have come from the skill with which stock tenders cracked their whips."[1]

---

[1] *Florida The Land Of Romance*; Dr. Dorothy Dodd, Florida State Librarian, Published by: Department of Agriculture, Tallahassee, Florida, The Peninsular Publishing Co. Tallahassee, 1957. Pages 62-63

By 1881, Florida had 550 miles of railroads. The Florida lines attracted the attention of men such as Henry B. Plant and Henry M. Flagler. This new transportation feature gave rise to new settlements and livestock pens at rail side. They then connected with Jacksonville and the northern markets.

In 1898, the Spanish American war created another market for the railroads to ship soldiers to Tampa and cattle to Cuba to feed the soldiers from the same port of embarkation.

This story developed during these times and before as the Patriarch of this story came to the central Florida area shortly after being mustered out of the Army of the United States of America.

His cattle business grew from a few scrub cows pried loose from unforgiving terrain, using only two cur catch dogs and the horse which was given to him at the end of the war as part of his final pay. He was allowed to keep his Spencer repeater and his single action army Colt pistol.

He literally scratched out a place in history by being one of the first cattle barons in central Florida. As he advanced in age, his legacy needed new blood. It came to him in the form of two rough but honest cracker cowboys, an engineer surveyor, and a Seminole Indian hunting party that always camped near the hammock.

Although the names are fictitious, much of the storyline is created around actual places that existed during and after the story. Lake Wailes became Lake Wales; Fort Blount became Bartow; Fort Cummins became Lake Alfred; and the Star settlement became Avon Park and of course, Fort Meade is still known as Fort Meade.

The hammock which is written about was between Thompson Nursery Road, in the south, the Dundee road (Fl 542) north, and U.S. 27 on the east.

Until recently, the cow pens were still evident as well as the little graveyard. Now, however, there is a huge apartment complex growing on the site. The sad thing is, there is no longer the wilderness or the beauty of the Bent Penny Cow Pens.

CRACKERS IN THE SCRUB
CHARACTER CHART

Jeremiah Coxin:	He is a forty year old illiterate cowboy who dresses in blue jeans, a cotton shirt with a bandana and an old Stetson hat with a dark sweat band. He is five feet nine inches tall and has character in the wrinkles in his face. He rides an old gelding roan with an arrowhead blaze. His horse stands at thirteen hands and is still a good cow pony.
Earl Ray Remmick:	He is five feet seven inches tall and baldheaded except for a tuft of hair above his ears and down the back of his head. He dresses in old blue jeans with a shirt made from a flour sack. A red bandana is around his neck, and a straw hat sits on his head. His horse is a Marsh Tacky which has four white stocking legs and has on a converted McClelland saddle. Earl is shy around people; however, he is an expert with his bull whip and usually follows Jeremiah's suggestions.

David Crocket Pierce:	Educated with some college credits, David is from Brunswick, Georgia and surveys for the railroad. He wears light tan riding breeches and shirt, with a hat in the form of a pith helmet, and high-top, lace-up boots. At first, he is unaccustomed to being around cattle but learns quickly from Jeremiah and Earl Ray. Later, he graduates from the University of Georgia and earns his engineering degree from Massachusetts Institute of Technology.
Mr. Allbritton:	He is an older man with wrinkles in his face which give him the appearance of a permanent smile. He served as a colonel in the Army of the United States of America and is married to Sue Lynn De Mott. They have one child, Becky. They moved from Jacksonville, Florida after the Civil War. He started the Bent Penny Cow Pens where the ranchers and cowboys bring their scrub cows to be herded to market. He owns the land through a land grant from the federal government and has created a business of buying and driving cattle to the market. He is a firm, honest man who treats everyone well. He wears mostly cotton trousers with a plaid shirt and vest. His cowboy boots are new and well kept. His hair is salt and pepper with longer hair in the back around his collar. He rides a Marsh Tacky horse given to him by the Seminole Indians.

Old Will Henry:	He is a tall, well-built Negro man who is employed by David Pierce's survey company. He works hard and is very strong. He wears the old uniforms from the surveyors and boots that are from the cavalry. He drives the survey wagon and maintains Pierce's survey company.
Mary Sykes Remmick:	She is a large lady but not fat and is five feet five inches tall. She was married but is a widow and cooks and cleans house for Mr. Allbritton. Mary is good at sewing, mending and first aid. She also keeps books and writes letters for Mr. Allbritton. Firm but kind to the workers, she is totally dedicated to her job at Bent Penny Cow Pens. Later, she marries Earl Ray Remmick.
Mr. Bodow:	He is a Jewish fellow who runs the emporium and general store in the town of Kissimmee, Florida. He has several businesses which he runs from his store. He knows almost all the ranchers and cowboys in the area.
Mrs. Wampler	She is a very large woman who is a great cook and runs the boarding house in Kissimmee with an iron hand. She is very jovial and titters when she laughs.

Mrs. Leona Petty:	She is the seamstress who makes shirts and dresses for the cowboys and the ladies in the Kissimmee area. Her shop is across the street from the general store.
Willie Mae Luke:	She is the housekeeper for Mary Sykes after Mary marries Earl Ray Remmick. She is the wife of John Henry Luke and is a small Negro lady who can not bare children. She is a good cook and is accustomed to cooking for large groups.
John Henry Luke:	He is a very big Negro man who stands six feet and weighs about three hundred pounds. He can lift a two hundred pound anvil above his head and can throw a horse or mule to the ground. He drives the wagon and buggy for Mr. Allbritton, chops wood for the stove and the fireplaces in the compound, tends the kitchen garden, and does other odd jobs around the cow pens.
Tom Walker:	He is a cow hand who drifts into the area and is hired by Mr. Allbritton to help with the notching, cutting and general duties around the cow pens. He is in his mid-thirties when he arrives at Bent Penny, however, his dark sun-tanned skin makes him look like he is much older. His floppy hat shows sweat marks from its many years of wear. He marries Orange Blossom and adopts her child, Little Billy. They later have another child, a girl whom they name Mary after Mary Remmick.

Cliff Teague:	He is somewhat like Tom who drifts into the compound and is hired to be a cowboy and perform other duties around the cow pens. He shows his forty-two years and walks with pronounced bowed legs. They often tease him about his bowlegs by saying, "Cliff, you couldn't hem up a pig in a ditch." He never marries but spends all his latter years at the Bent Penny Cow Pens.
Orange Blossom:	She is a Seminole woman who stays with a scrub cowboy until she gets pregnant. Then, he casts her out and so do her people. She has the baby in the scrub and is found by the crackers from Bent Penny. After that, she and Tom Walker fall in love and are married.
Wendell Hampton:	He is a long time friend of Mr. Allbritton. They were in the Civil War together and became fast friends after he saved Wendell's life. He marries into wealth and becomes the owner of the Holt Industries in Savannah, Georgia.
Mary Ellen Hampton:	She is the wife of Wendell Hampton. Her father owned Holt Industries before his death when Mary's daughter was only seven years old. She is of the Savannah aristocracy, a southern belle and a debutante. She marries Wendell Hampton when she is twenty years old and has her daughter when she is twenty-two.

Brittany Hampton:	She is the daughter of Wendell and Mary Ellen Hampton, who has just turned eighteen and will be enrolled in college at Milledgeville, Georgia, in the coming fall. She was a debutante at age sixteen and was given her first horse for her coming out gift. Perky and a bit spoiled, she is the apple of her father's eye.
Billy Mason:	He is a mule skinner and teamster who drives freight to Florida and finds that the Sanford area is the most lucrative market for his expertise. He hires on to drive the wagon with the barrels of gifts given to Mr. Allbritton by the Hampton's. He stays on as a freighter for Bent Penny's salt business and brings cow and horse feed from Kissimmee and Tampa.
Bob Tacket:	Bob is a close friend of David Crocket Pierce, who graduated with Davy from the University of Georgia where they were roommates for most of the university days. He later goes into business with Davy. Their surveying company's business is run by Bob while Davey does all the field work with his survey crew.
Billy Wilcox:	He is the adopted son of Tom who marries Orange Blossom after Billy is born in the scrub. He is an olive skin lad with the true features of a Seminole. His dark eyes, eyebrows and hair seem to shine like a rainbow with its many changing colors in the sunlight.

David Pierce, Jr.:	David is the first-born twin of Brittany and David Crocket Pierce and is fifteen minutes older than his brother Johnny. The blond hair and blue eyes are a dead give away that he, like his brother, are the sons of Davy and Brittany Pierce.
Johnny Pierce:	He is the second son and other twin of the Pierce household. Johnny, like his brother, has blond hair and blue eyes. They are identical in every way except to be mirrored, as David seems to favor his right hand and Johnny his left.
Bent Penny Cow Pens:	The compound is in a large oak and hickory hammock, and the land is clear where the cow pens and the pastures are. There are several buildings on the compound: the main house and office, the bunk house, the barn and corral for the horses, the tack shed, hay barn, dog pens, feed lot, and two large areas for feeding the hands. One is inside the main house where long tables are set up and the food is placed on the tables to pass to each other. In the summer when the weather is hot, the same type of set up is under an open shed with tables where the hands have to stand to eat. There is a well and spring house. Also, there are a smoke house and several sheds for getting out of the heat and sun when working on rolling stock and the smithy. Later, a one-room schoolhouse is built on the foundation of the dance floor which was erected earlier for a special event.

Mc Gorkles Saloon:	This is a seedy bar in Ft. Meade with dirt floors and a bar made of wooden planks laid across two barrels. This place is where cracker cowboys vent their long days in the scrub. Also, Mc Gorkles is where alcohol and loose women vie for the crackers' money. Killings, cuttings and all sorts of mayhem run rampant and unchecked in the saloon at the crossroads that lead to Tampa and Punta Rassa cattle shipping ports.
Marsh Tacky:	A Marsh Tacky is a small saddle horse that is 13 to 15 hands high at the withers and is sought by cracker cowboys for its ability to move through the scrub and anticipate the movement of Florida scrub cows. It is as fast as a quarter horse and agile enough to keep herds moving or bunched for driving. They are not big or heavy enough for roping; so most cowboys own a roping horse or mule to complete the tools of his trade needed to round up, drive, and brand scrub cattle. There is a remuda of 10 to 12 Marsh Tackies at the Bent Penny Ranch. They are so much in demand that Mr. Allbritton starts buying from and trading with the Seminole Indians for the horses they can find and break to saddle. At this time and date the Marsh Tackies are coming from nearby and from the Everglades. Each year, they are becoming scarcer.

Catch Dogs:	Catch dogs are generally cur dogs that are of no particular breed. They are not fed, as a rule, by anyone except the owner. They are loyal and gentle, but fierce foes of the scrub cow and can catch and throw a cow on their own.
Chief Billy Bow Legs:	Though the original Chief Billy Bowlegs died in 1877, he had two wives; and this man, Young Tiger Tail as he was called while growing up, was raised by the second wife after his mother died from the measles. He changes his name to Billy Bow Legs when he is 18 and becomes a Seminole Warrior. His band of about 12 to 50 men, women, and children, range and hunt from Kissimmee to Ft. Meade. They make their winter camp on Billy Bow Legs Creek just east of Ft. Meade. They hunt cattle and horses in the scrub and farm by growing pumpkins, gourds, sugar cane, and various vegetables and berries. They round up and break to saddle the Marsh Tacky horses which are the wild horses from the Spanish Conquistadors. The horses were either lost or abandoned when the Spanish seceded Florida to the French in 1719 A.D. As stated above, Chief Bow Legs the son of the last great chief of the Seminole Indians who is famous because he would not leave Florida when President Andrew Jackson made the Indians travel the "Trail of Tears." He camped between Ft. Meade and Avon Park (the Star Settlement) on what is now Bill Bow Legs Creek.

CHAPTER ONE

CRACKERS IN THE SCRUB

In 1878, Jeremiah Coxin had drifted from the Texas Panhandle to the plains of Oklahoma, working cattle all the while. Oil fields began replacing cattle ranches, so the cattle industry moved north to Montana. He decided that the weather in Montana was not suitable to the warmth he needed for his aching cowboy bones.

He started working his way south and eventually found himself in the center of Georgia. This was 1891 and Jeremiah had just turned twenty-eight. Things were beginning to grow from the shipping of cotton and tobacco to the north. The hustle and bustle of Milledgeville, Georgia became more than he wanted to be around.

Jeremiah talked to a steamboat captain who told him, "As soon as this trip is over, I'm going to head down to Florida. They say that they are shipping cattle from Tampa and Punta Rassa to Cuba to the Cuban army. They have a war going on down there now, and I might as well get some of that Spanish gold."

Jeremiah was building his campfire at the edge of town when a lanky man rode up on a horse that seemed to have seen better days many years before this meeting.

"Y'all got notion ta let a stranger share yer far there in tha camp?" His drawl gave him away. Another Texan.

"Shore light down an brang any fixin's whut ya got." Jeremiah called back to the man.

Soon a roaring fire was going and the coffee pot was blowing out the aroma of fresh coffee as it can smell only at a campfire.

Jeremiah stuck out his hand and said, "Ah'm Jeremiah Coxin; ah done come from Oklahoma from Texas. The oil done runt tha cow business and I wonts ta see what tha east looked lack."

The man took his hand and shook it, then said, "Earl Ray Remmick, I jist bout did the same thang cept'n ah come from San Antone ta here. I done gone by ta Naw'lens, an the sights ah done seen… well sir I hain't gonna see nuthin lack at ayre agin, no sir." Then added, "Ah got some pone stones an bac'n we'uns kin fry up. I ain't had no time ta soak the pone stones today, but mebe we kin fry then long side with the bac'n and they be tol'able ta eat crisp."

That was the beginning of a life-long partnership of two like hearts that wanted to travel and see what adventures lurked around the next bend in the trail.

"Ah'm a gonna go ta Flar'dy, Earl Ray. If you an me kin hit it off, then we'uns mount wont ta be thar the same. Ah bespoke ta a river captain, and he said they was a drivin cow critters ta a place called Pump sumthin and a place name o Tampa. They was a sendin them cow critters ta a place what was at war and needs cow ta feed them soldiers. So come mawnin ah'm a headed south ta Flar'dy."

After two months of travel (mostly walking for both had the old US Army issue McClelland saddles that were easy on the horses but not on the back-side of the cowboys that used them for their work), they walked and rode around swamps, lakes, crossed a prairie and came to the St. Johns River. They worked for two days to get fifteen cents to pay the ferryboat toll across for themselves and the two horses.

Now here they are in central Florida at a lake called Lake Wailes and have been hunting scrub cows with their whips, catch dogs and with horses not suited for the rigors of the Florida scrub.

They have driven several dozen cows from the scrub and fought oak thickets, palmettos as high as a man's head on horse back, cabbage palms, gall berry bushes and thick white sand as white as sugar. And now, they have put into an oak and hickory hammock with the inside being a cypress swamp. As it begins to get twilight, the frogs in the cypress pond start singing their nightly songs to any who will listen.

The evening is on them, and with the precaution on range savvy cowboys they hear in the distance a noise of movement in the scrub...

"Dang! I hate a cold camp," said Jeremiah

"Yeah, even in Flar'dy hit seems cold when y'all cain't have no far to cook er jist to keep a body comp'ny," answered Earl Ray.

"Shhhh, ah kin hear sumpum in ta tha brush," Jeremiah warned.

"Is hit a commin this-away?" asked Earl Ray.

"Cain't tell yet. Hits still too fer over yonder I recon," whispered Jeremiah.

The warm summer Florida night in July 1895 seemed to be darker than usual, and under the oak trees in the hammock there was little starlight for objects to be silhouetted against the horizon. The palmettos were almost head high just outside the clearing of the hammock. Yet a good alarm system let it be known that something was moving; however it was difficult to tell if it was a cow or a horse, maybe with a man astraddle. Just too many unknowns to suit these Florida crackers.

Jeremiah Coxin and Earl Ray Remmick had been rounding up scrub cows in the Blue scrub about thirty miles south and east of Fort Blount. The cows were getting harder to find, and it took the cowboys fifteen or twenty days longer this roundup than in the past few years.

"I shore wousht hit was daylight, Jeremiah," Earl Ray said in a whisper which could have been heard in a sawmill."

"We need ta keep ourn backs ta tha big oaks. You git over yonder, and you look a from my back and ah'll look to yoren," Jeremiah told Earl Ray.

The cowboys each had a Winchester 92 in .45-caliber long colt and a single action army revolver in the same caliber. Therefore, they only had to keep up with one caliber of ammunition. The colts were always carried with the hammer down on an empty chamber. This was to prevent any embarrassing discharges in case the pistol was dropped. This night, however, they felt the cylinder until the empty chamber came into the loading position in the loading gate. A cartridge was quietly loaded into the chamber and the pistol readied for whatever was coming through the palmetto scrub.

The silence of the night was torn out of reason when the palmettos rustled, and the sound was now just yards away from the men in the hammock. A flock of birds flew up and chirped their displeasure at being rudely interrupted from their slumber by this invasive intrusion into the roosting area. As the animal broke into the clearing, the horse snorted and was answered by cowboys' horses which were hobbled over by the edge of the swamp.

With the surprise of the horses' neigh and snort, the strange horse shied back toward the scrub.

Then Jeremiah and Earl Ray heard a man say, "Somebody's in there, and if you don't tell me who, I might start shooting in those woods and y'all might not make it to morning."

"We kin see you'ens a heep bettern you kin see us, so you jist light down from that hoss, and if you know whut's good fer ya and that hoss, keep walking standin up or I'll kill yore hoss and my partner will kill you," Jeremiah ordered.

"Ok, ok, I'm gitting down now. Don't shoot me," the stranger said.

"Now lead that hoss on in ta tha hammock. I'll tell ya when ta stop," Jeremiah added.

The stranger dismounted and led the horse toward the voice.

"Ok, that's fer enough. Ease down on the ground and start a far in front o' ya," Jeremiah continued.

"I can't see a thing in here! How am I supposed to build a fire if I can't see to find wood?" the stranger moaned.

"Jist git down on yore hands and knees and feel fer some," Jeremiah said.

The man dropped to his knees, and they could hear him rustling through the leaves feeling for sticks or limbs to use for a fire. Occasionally, he let out a mild oath especially when he stuck his hand on a prickly pear cactus.

The man piled whatever he could find by feeling around on the ground, then he said, "Don't have any matches to light the fire."

"Earl Ray, y'all keep yore Winchester aimed at him while I go and light the far fer ishere tenderfoot fool. No matches, how never will ya survive these woods thowt no a way ta start a far?" Jeremiah mused as he crept over toward the man's voice.

Jeremiah struck the match with the thumbnail of his left hand as the colt was in his right hand. The match flamed with what seemed to be a thousand lightning strikes inside that hammock. Even though it blinded the stranger, it blinded Jeremiah, too. So for a few seconds, he looked away from the flame and cocked the pistol at the same time. If the stranger wanted to jump Jeremiah in the flash of the match, he thought better of it when he heard the hammer being cocked on that colt.

Jeremiah quickly struck the burning match into a pile of leaves and told the man to, "Put the small twigs on the far first. Then, when that's cotched up afar, start putten on the bigger branches."

Soon there was enough fire for the cowboys to see that the stranger was dressed like a dude from some place other than the Florida scrub.

"Who are you and what ayre ya doing out cheer in the middle of no whars and how come you ayre a wanderin round ish here scrub in tha night time?" Earl Ray finally spoke out, surprising the man. As yet, he wasn't sure there were two of them. Now with doubt put to rest, he settled in to tell them his story.

"Well you see, I am with a survey party out of Brunswick, Georgia. We are surveying the land that has been granted to the railroad by the federal government, and I had the duty to hunt for wild game for our evening meal. And as you now know I really got lost. I thought I heard cows lowing, and I followed the sound until I really knew I was hopelessly lost in the scrub. When night fell, I couldn't find a suitable place to camp. I literally stumbled upon your camp and thought I was dead when your horses snorted and neighed. I was bluffing about shooting at you. I don't even have a gun. I've got a machete and an ax but no gun."

"How were ya gonna kill no game thout no gun?" Earl Ray asked.

"Old Will Henry was with me. He had the gun, but we got separated. Now, I'm just about as tired as a man can get and still move." The man said.

"Well I rec'con y'all muss be done good'n hongery by now, too, I rec'con. We had a cold camp cause we heered you a comin thew that scrub for a mile or two." Jeremiah sighed.

Earl Ray was already headed back to the campfire with bacon, beans and some pone stones. The pone stones were small dollar-sized cornbread made of bacon grease, corn meal, flour, salt and water. When fried in bacon fat, they stayed edible for about three days. Then they got harder and harder until they had to be soaked in water and fried again to be edible.

The men ate a good supper, the stranger especially. Earl Ray touted, "Do all y'all surveyors eat like you do? Yew et lack you hain't et in a week, Mr... what is yore name any way?"

"David Crocket Pierce," the man said. He felt relieved now that they knew his name. They might help him find his way back to the area on Lake Wailes where he last saw his party.

"David Crocket?" Earl Ray and Jeremiah said at the same time. Then Earl Ray added, "Why, ole Davy Crocket muss be a rollin in hissens graveyard iffen he knowed somebody with hissen name was lost in the Flar'dy scrub." They all three laughed and joked at the expense of the tenderfoot whom they had apparently rescued from a fatal mistake.

The cattle lowed at the break of day and caused a stir in the camp. All three men sat up from their sleep, stretched, yawned and stood up to greet the new day.

Earl Ray went to his saddle, opened the saddle bag took out a mailorder catalog and tore out two pages, walked into the palmetto scrub. Meanwhile, Jeremiah and Davy lit the fire and put on the coffee pot. Jeremiah sliced three slabs of bacon and dropped it into the cast iron skillet which shared the fire with the coffee pot. The coffee was starting to boil and the aroma of bacon cooking and coffee almost ready to pour made the hammock have a feature of home, sweet home.

"That sure does smell good," Davy uttered, and he broke another piece of firewood and placed it on the fire.

"Good god! Yeeow!" yelled Earl Ray as he came running back into the clearing with his trousers in tow trying not to trip as he called, "Jeremiah bring the gun and come a runnin..."

Jeremiah knowing that Earl Ray wasn't a man to be alarmed about nothing, grabbed the colt pistol and met Earl Ray who was strangely white where no sun got to his body and said to Jeremiah, "There is one big rattler in there, and I were eyeball to eyeball with at critter. He didn't even rattle until I yelled then, he cut a chatter."

Jeremiah just grinned and started toward the snake which was still rattling. Soon, a resounding bang echoed, and the rattling stopped. Jeremiah came back into the clearing with the rattler dragging behind him. It was nearly six feet long and was as big around as his thigh.

"Great day, look at the size of that thing!" Davy said and went to get a closer look.

"Earl Ray you git yoreself cleaned up and skin this critter so's we kin have fried rattler fer breakfast," Jeremiah said as he drove a spike into an oak tree and hung the snake on the spike for Earl Ray to skin.

The edible part of the snake was cut into strips and washed in fresh water, then salted, dredged with corn meal and fried in the bacon grease.

After breakfast was over Davy went to the edge of the swamp where there was now a pool of water made there by the horses stamping their feet at the water's edge during the night to drink. The dishes were done and the coffee pot was now boiling water so the men would have clean water to drink during the ride and, if need be, for supper that night.

"Well Davy, did you never herd cow critters afore?" Earl Ray asked.

"No I never did, but something tells me I'm about to learn," he answered, "I'll just about do anything to get back to civilization and my main party."

"Ok then, saddle up and let's find out how fer them cow critters wandered last night and if that snake shot went and run em off any," Earl Ray said as he mounted his horse.

The whip cracked as they headed the cows into a circle. Jeremiah was on one side of the circle and Earl Ray on the other, while Davy was riding drag to keep the cows from moving away from the herd.

Two whips cracked, and the cows started moving at a slow pace toward Lake Wailes.

"Along about dinner we ought to count up and see if we got a rock bag full yet," Jeremiah said.

The rock bags were leather bags with a certain number of rocks in one bag. They were about the same size and weight. The bags were different colors, and when they counted each cow, a rock was taken from one bag and placed into another. When the rocks were completely out

7

of the first bag, then they drove the cows to the cow pens. Since most of the crackers were illiterate, this is how the count was assured, and every cow buyer would accept the rock bag count. At Bent Penny Cow Pens, a cattle buyer would pay for the cows that the cracker cowboys had rounded up from the woods and scrub in the area, then drive them to the shipping point. The closest was in Tampa, a week's drive west. There the cows were loaded on steamboats to be taken around the tip of Florida to the northeast markets, or south to Cuba.

CHAPTER TWO

THE HURRICANE

At noon, when the Florida sun forbade any activity that day, the men were in the shade of a live oak tree. The cow count had begun.

"Jist a lookin at em don't peer ta be no bag full yet, Jeremiah," Earl Ray said. He pushed his straw hat back to wipe the sweat from his brow and bald head. "Hit shore got hot in the scrub today. Thank we is in fer a blow this evening?"

Jeremiah scanned the sky and said, "Hit shore do look lack hits a building over the west. I rec'con we ought to go ahead an move'm t'ard Bent Penny Pens...Did ja heer that hit? Seemed lack thunder over yonder," he added, "Less us weigh the rock bag and see iffen we got a pistol weight yet."

A colt single action revolver with six rounds in the cylinder weighs about two pounds. The sack would be strung up one end of a long straight stick and the colt on the other end. A string in the middle of the stick created a primitive balance of sorts. If the rocks were as heavy as the gun, then they had approximately 300 cows or a half a bag of rocks representing that many cows.

"When y'all gonna have that railroad built Davy?" Earl Ray asked as he cracked his whip, and they began heading the cows to the west and north.

Davy answered, "I really don't know. We've only surveyed about twenty miles of the federal land grant to the railroad, and it's supposed to run from Jacksonville down to Sanford, then across the St. Johns River to the Orange Settlement, then to Fort Cummins. Our section is from Ft. Cummins to Ft. Blount, then all the way to Ft. Meade. We'll have loading pens at Ft. Cummins and at Ft. Meade. That will relieve the Tampa port stockyards for more cattle coming up from the grass river area down south to the big Lake Okeechobee. There are still a lot of scrub cows in that area."

"Earl Ray, yew rec'con we kin make it to the turpentine camp on Lake Wailes today? Iffen hit blows, I shore would lack ta have these cow critters in a corral of some kind," Jeremiah said.

As the afternoon wore on, the clouds thickened and became angry black. Lightning struck the tall pine trees, and the cattle spooked more with each ensuing thunder clap. On the east side of Lake Wailes, they could see the turpentine still across the lake; it was a two hour drive to get to the corral.

Luckily they noticed that there were some slash pine cabins which had been hastily built in the last two or three weeks since Jeremiah and Earl Ray had been through there on their way to the scrub.

A large bolt of lightning struck a pine a few hundred feet from the men, and they saw ten head of cows struck dead from electrocution. Jeremiah and Earl Ray spurred their mounts up and raced to the dead cows. Then as fast as they could run from one to another, slit their throats to let them bleed out. They would come back later and butcher them or drag them to the camp and let the folks in the camp have some fresh beef.

After the cows' throats were cut, the three men abandoned the rest of the herd and ran their mounts to the camp. As they rode into the camp, the clouds released the rain, soaking the men to the skin in seconds. They tied the horses under a lean-to shed and ran for another shed where the turpentine still was shaded from the Florida sun. This shelter was now a haven to the three nearly drowned men.

"Rec'con I hain't gonna hafta take me no bath this Sattiddy," Earl Ray quipped.

"No, nor me neether," said Jeremiah.

Davy spoke up and said, "If it slacks up some, we can go down to my cabin and wait this out."

"Why in sam hill didn't we'uns jist keep a goin til we come ta yore cabin, Davy? Now we gonna git all wet again. Well why don't we jist git on over to yore cabin Davy and we can take longer to dry out," Jeremiah said.

So another mad dash was under way as the three men trotted toward the last cabin in the row of six and burst through the door.

There was a folding canvas cot in one corner, a table and chair under the only window in the cabin, and a table with a coal oil camp stove and an oil lamp at the other end of the cabin. The cabin was only 12 feet by 12 feet with a slash roof that kept most of the rain out. The white sugar-sand floor drank the water up as it leaked in through the slash roof.

Jeremiah and Earl Ray found a dry corner and squatted down on the floor. Davy sat on his canvas cot.

The rain seemed to come harder and harder, and the wind was howling through the pines outside making the small cabin rock more and more with each gust of wind. Then there was a crack, and a piece of the roof disappeared, then another and another. As Davy moved toward the same corner with Jeremiah and Earl Ray, what was left of the roof blew away. The men huddled in the corner as the wind took the door and window. The cabin buckled and slowly settled over the three men, making a solid pine lean-to that was propped up by the two tables. The rain was not getting to them as the wind was blowing the rain in sheets from west to east. Then the tall pines began twisting as the storm tore the tops from the trees, dropping them some 500 yards away and into the lake. The wind blew and blew for about two hours, and the lake was now inching its way toward the camp.

Suddenly, the wind calmed down to a gentle breeze and since darkness was settling in, the men quickly went to look after the mounts. They had taken time to unsaddle them and sling the saddles over the top rail of the fence.

The three men stopped in total amazement to see that Davy's cabin was the only one left by the storm. The turpentine shed was gone; the still was in several pieces; and the large kettle vat was quickly becoming inundated by the lake water. Trees were blown down; tops were missing;

the shed where they had left the mounts was gone; yet saddles were still intact on the top fence rail. There was no sign of the horses, but on around the lake shore a few hundred yards was a large water oak which had lost some limbs and was stripped almost bare of Spanish moss and leaves. They heard a snort and knew that the riding stock had most likely wandered to the next best shelter.

The trio looked for other signs of life but there was no one else in the camp.

"I wonder war ever body is at," Jeremiah said, "Most lackly they's gone to the coat house and the church at Ft. Blount."

Then he almost shouted, "What is that roarin sound a comin from the east?" They all looked at the same time to see a solid wall of rain headed for them from across the lake. He hastily added, "We best git whatever logs we can to shore up the cabin cause the thing has turned around and is headed back fer us."

The three men quickly picked up any siding they could find to place in the front of the now lean-to cabin. They hurriedly placed as many boards as they could. By the time they were safe inside their haven, the wind and rain returned with a vengeance. The wind shook the newly placed boards, but somehow they held. The men just waited until the wind stopped, but it kept on raining until midday of the next day.

Now, cold and wet, the survivors started fetching pine limbs, boards and oak limbs that had blown down. Using the coal oil from the tank of the camp stove, they started a roaring fire and kept the fire going until the following day.

The threesome had not eaten now for almost three days and figured that the pone stones were most likely too wet to eat, much less to re-cook. The bacon was no doubt spoiled, but there was a good thing that could come from the dousing they had taken. The beans should be well soaked and that would make them cook faster.

Earl Ray walked over to the saddles and looked inside the saddle bag. He grinned a broad grin and sauntered back to the fire with the skillet, dry beans, pone stones, and the bacon wrapped up in the oil paper as good as new.

"Well we'uns ain't got no head start on the beans, but if we bile'm long nuff we kin still eat some in the morning fer breakfast. Maybe

Jeremiah will kill us another rattler. The other'n went down purtty good, don't cha know," Earl Ray finished.

They saddled the horses and rode back to where they had bled the cows killed by the lightning only to find them bloated and useless to anything but the buzzards. They rode back to the camp and started foraging for any food that they might find in what was left of the camp. They all came back with various canned goods; however, the rain had washed away most of the labels and Davy said, "We are really going to have a potluck supper tonight."

The next morning, the sounds of horses and wagons was heard coming through the storm-flattened scrub. As they approached, Davy recognized the survey wagon and Old Will Henry driving. When the wagons pulled up and stopped, Will Henry climbed down and stuck out his hand to Davy.

Will Henry said, "I sho thot y'all was a goner mista Davy. I hollard and hollard fer ye tuther day, but when dark come on, I knowed gee was lost in the scrub. We'uns was gonna go looking fer ye but the storm started up and so we'uns went to Ft. Cummins. Y'all know what… they's a railroad to Ft. Cummins now. Yep, they's jist built er and the train will come there next week."

Will Henry looked around and made a tisking sound after surveying the area where the turpentine camp and the cabins, that were hastily erected for shelter and work area for the surveyors, were no longer imposing on the white sands of the lake shore. With unbelieving eyes, he whistled and said, "Ain't much lef o' dis here place. Who dat lean-to belong to?"

Davy answered, "That's what's left of my cabin, Will Henry. All the others were blown away or down, so we used most of what was left for fire wood. The vat to the still is yonder in the lake, and it's going to be a monster of a job getting that big thing back on its foundation again. My drawings are ruined, but I still have my field book so I can redraw them. It'll just take some time."

Will Henry asked, "Who be them fellers? Did tha storm blow them in too?

Davy chuckled, "No, Will Henry, they actually saved my life. I was lucky to run up on them and after a rocky start, they took me under their wing. We drove their cattle here to the east side of the lake. After that storm, I have no idea that these men will find all those cows again. Lightning killed ten of them, and we tried to save the meat. But the storm drove us away. So the meat went to spoil… maybe when the rest of the crew gets here we can all go and help Jeremiah and Earl Ray round up those cows again. It'll take them until next summer to get them bunched up by themselves."

As the afternoon wore on to early evening, the camp was again abuzz with men sitting up tents and gathering fire wood for the supper meal. The folks from Ft. Cummins had given them enough supplies to get things started again, and with six mules in the harness, the vat was almost back to its foundation.

Six men rebuilt Davy's cabin and it was ready for the trio to sleep in that night. The tables were okay in spite of the fact that they held up one wall of the cabin through the storm.

A roaring fire was going on into the night as the men worked to get the still back in service. For there were a lot of trees which were tapped, and the pine sap needed to be cooked off into tar, pitch and turpentine.

Jeremiah and Earl Ray had brought the horses up and tied them to the rail fence which dutifully held the saddles all during the tempest. They curried and combed the pine needles, oak leaves and moss from their mains and tails. Soon they were fed oats and corn which was brought in from Ft. Cummins.

Earl Ray said, "That ole hoss wont wanna leave after all them good vittles y'all feedin er. When she gits hungry nuff tho, I rec'con she'll eat that scrub grass and drink swamp water jist lack she ust ta."

After a day at the turpentine camp, Jeremiah and Earl Ray were saying good-bye to Davy when a group of men rode up on horses and mules.

Davy said, "We're going to help you find your cows so you can get them to the pens and get your money."

"We're bliged to you, and we shore kin use the hep. Tell y'all what… let's move out in a line and circle back from the hammock to the lake. There oughta be near three hundred head scattered out there. And look for two notches in the lef ear. Ats ar mark."

In a day's time, the cows were moving to the cracking of whips through the camp, and Jeremiah was moving rocks from one bag to the other. When he ran out of rocks and the bag was empty, the cows were still coming.

Jeremiah called to Davy, "I hain't got no more rocks; y'all musta come up with seven or eight hundred head. Yew shore they hain't got sum nother mark?"

Davy laughed and said, "You all don't give my survey crew and the distillers much truck as far as cowboys do you?"

"I ain't lookin no gift cow in the mouth. I'm gonna thank y'all, and if you will give me a count there, Davy, I shore preshate it," Jeremiah said.

Davy said, "You got eight hundred fifty-seven ole scrub cows... now you want us to help you drive them to the Bent Penny Cow Pens?"

Earl Ray spoke up and said, "Iffin we'uns cud jist two of yur men we'd be mighty bliged to y'all, Davy."

"You've got them. Now when do you want to start the drive?" asked Davey.

"At sun up. So we'll have breakfast at fo thuty and be a headin up at sun up. Yessir at sun up," Jeremiah said. "Now let's turn in and git sum shut eye. Hits a gonna be a long three day."

The three days were mostly uneventful, and when the Bent Penny Cow Pens were in view, Jeremiah rode on ahead and came into the clearing, got down and walked to the house. There was a sign hanging by chains that read "OFFICE." Jeremiah knocked on the door.

A portly woman answered and said, "Yes, what can we do for you?"

Jeremiah took off his hat and rolled the brim, then cleared his throat and said, "Is Mista Allbritton to home Ma'am? I got nigh on ta... nigh on ta eight hundred and fifty head o cows a comin in, and I wish Mista Allbritton would look em over. They's good cows and their clean after the storm don cha know. Er..ah..my name's Jeremiah Coxin, ma'am. I'm kinda the ram rod too."

"Wait there," the woman said, "I'll get him."

A man most of six feet tall came to the door. He was tan from many days and months in the Florida sun, and his wrinkles gave a character to his face like nothing Jeremiah had seen in a man during his lifetime. "How many head you got?" Mister Allbritton asked.

"Well, we got the rock bag and two hundred fifty more 'cordin ta the survey man's count. He writ them all down on ishere paper. Ever one is writ down now. Here's the rock bags and tha paper Davy, tha survey man, writ."

"Ok, bring them on in to the pens, and I'll count the rock after supper... You all will be joining us for supper, won't you? How many drover are with you?"

Jeremiah put his hat back on his head, so his hands would be free for him to count on his fingers.

"Well, sir, there's mu partner Earl Ray, and a black man name a Will Henry, and Mista David Crocket Pierce. Yessir, there's that many," and he held up four fingers.

"Very good, now go and open the gates for the cows. Then, when you are all done, you can wash up for supper, straight away," Mr. Allbritton ordered.

The cows went in the pens, and the men ate a ranch hand's supper of roast beef, boiled potatoes, collard greens, black-eye peas, corn bread and for desert, pecan pie, with coffee to wash it all down with.

"That was a shore good supper Ma'am," Earl Ray said. "I hain't had vittles lack unto them since I was a boy ta home."

"Well, it's good to see men eat and enjoy a meal like you all did tonight. Now if you don't want anything else to eat, get out of the kitchen so I can clean up," the woman fussed.

"I'll shore be glad to hep you with the dishes for another slice o that there peacan pie, Ma'am; I shore will, too," Earl Ray volunteered.

"I don't need a fumble-fingered man breaking my china. Now you just skedaddle out of here and help the other boys count the cows," the woman scolded, "but when you're finished, the pie will be waiting on the pie safe. Just help yourself."

Mr. Allbritton walked into his office and sat down at a roll-top desk and with a key opened the desk and removed a strong box. He asked, "Do you want cash or a bank draft which you can draw from any bank from Ft. Cummins to Kissimmee?"

Jeremiah looked at Earl Ray and then together they said, "Cash."

Mr. Allbritton wrote the amount in his ledger and the number of cows as he murmured to himself. That's eight hundred fifty-seven head at twelve dollars a head. That comes to... ten thousand, two hundred eighty-four dollars."

Jeremiah looked at Early Ray who had turned white at hearing such a large amount of money. Why, they never had more than twenty dollars, a month's pay for rounding up scrub cows, and now this had to be a king's ransom.

Mr. Allbritton broke into their thoughts to say, "Boys I don't have ten thousand dollars. Will you take a bank draft of the balance?"

"Yessir, we will. Would ya kindly make it out to Earl Ray Remmick. He lives sometimes in Kissimmee, and he kin draw on it there," Jeremiah spoke up, and Earl Ray agreed.

"Now, Mr. Allbritton, would you cipher as to how much that would be for the two of us?" Jeremiah asked.

"Sure, Jeremiah, that will be four thousand eight hundred fifty-eight dollars for Earl Ray plus the bank draft for two hundred eighty-four dollars to make a total of five thousand, one hundred forty-two dollars for each of you," said Mr. Allbritton.

"Thank you, Sir, and would you count out from each of ourn money a hundred dollars so's we kin give that much to Old Will Henry and Mista Davy the survey man?

"Why sure,...and I'll be glad to buy your cattle next spring too. Now you all put this money in a bank and let it draw interest for you," suggested Mr. Allbritton, "and if you will just sign or make your mark here in the ledger this deal will be finished."

"Thank you, Sir," the men said at the same time. They both made their own mark in the ledger, then shook hands and walked out of the office – rich men!

They were riding toward the turpentine camp when Earl Ray broke the silence. "Mista Davy, whot are interest?" Mr. Allbritton said to put this money in a bank soes hit could draw interest and we don't know whut hit means... interest."

Davy answered, "Well Earl Ray that is money that the bank pays you to let them use yours. It is usually paid to you once a year, but you can get shorter terms if you think you'll need the money before the year is out. Right now, I think that banks are paying two percent. That's two dollars for every hundred dollars you have in the bank."

"Oh…ah… how much can I keep for myself? I wont to buy some new clothes and boots. Then I would lack ta stay at a good hotel and eat store bought food in the café there. How much do you thank I'd need… ya know…altogether?" mused Earl Ray.

"That depends on how expensive your tastes are in clothes, food and the hotel," answered Davy, "Or you could not deposit the bank draft and let the merchant and hotel use what they need and they will give you back whatever is left over in change, don't you see."

"Ok…thanks Davy, I'll have to git ust ta be'in rich I guess," Earl Ray said as he rode on with the men to the camp.

Jeremiah and Earl Ray left the next morning and rode for three days to Ft. Blount. They heard a man by the name of Plant was building a railroad from Ft. Cummins to Tampa. They wondered if the man, David Crocket Pierce, the surveyor arithmetic whiz, ex-tenderfoot, and now cracker cowboy would be surveying that land, too.

"*CRACK*!" The whips report startled the horses.

Jeremiah asked, "Whut were that fer, Earl Ray? We ain't a droven no cows."

"Jist cause we be crackers in the scrub," Earl Ray answered.

CHAPTER THREE

BENT PENNY COW PENS

Earl Ray Remmick stepped out of Bodow's dry goods and general store onto the wooden sidewalk. The rough sawn lumber that was used to create the face on the old building was whitewashed and clean, but for the bit of trail dust that had lodged on the door and window frames. The large windows reflected the image of the main street, and it caught Earl Ray's eye as he walked in front and saw his full self in the window of Bodow's store. He was dressed to the nines with his new boots, pants, shirt, hat, bandana, belt with silver buckle, tooled leather suspenders, and Stetson hat. He even had on new long johns which itched a bit but were tolerable since he had had a warm bath, a shave, his hair trimmed, and had been sprinkled with talcum powder which smelled a bit like magnolia blossoms. The barber doused his freshly trimmed hair with hair tonic which was labeled "Lilac Water." Since Earl Ray was such a rich man from the last scrub cow round up and sale, he could ignore the side glances and sniffs as he met other folks walking along the sidewalk.

He walked into the hotel lobby which had had a dark red carpet. It covered the wooden floor like a bed of red grass, trimmed yet shaggy due to the many footsteps which tracked in sand, clay and even manure from the cows and horses. They had shamelessly left their fecal and urine waste on the ground which was stepped into by mistake. Earl Ray's glance met those of the hotel clerk and, through the wrought iron bars at the desk, asked the desk clerk for his key. The clerk, with a bit of a grin, asked him if such a distinguished gentleman was registered at this hotel.

Earl Ray lowered his head and blushed; this was the first time in his life he was called a gentleman.

"Yessir I'm signed here, and I have the room in the front upstairs," Earl Ray answered.

"Oh...oh yes, why you're Mr. Remmick in two-oh-five, aren't you?" the man quizzed. "My, my, you certainly do look different," he continued.

This time Earl Ray gave him a look of chagrin and asked, "What choo mean by that?"

"I...I just mean that you look so different...so good...like a gentleman and not like the cracker cowboy who came in here last night;" the clerk dodged the embarrassment of almost offending Earl Ray.

Earl Ray asked, "Do I really look lack a diff'rent man? I mean really?"

"Why Sir, you would pass for a rich, northern gentleman; and this hotel is honored to have you as a guest." The man looked seriously into Earl Ray's eye, nodding to embellish his flattery. Earl Ray gloated with pride.

Earl Ray walked away smiling as he thought about what the man had said and realized he was now in the café.

The waiter greeted him and asked if he would like a menu and something to drink. Each table had a clean white table cloth and four place settings. A condiment platter rested in the center of each table and kept handy the pepper vinegar, salt, pepper and a type of mustard prepared with vinegar and oil. There were even extra, white cotton napkins for the diner to use if he needed a frontal bib to save his clothes from spills.

As Earl Ray tried to look at the menu, the waiter politely took the menu from Earl Ray's hands, then turned it right side up. Earl Ray blushed again and looked at the menu, having no idea what it was that he was looking at; as he couldn't read or write even his name.

The waiter asked again, "Would you like something to drink, Sir?"
Earl Ray asked, "What choo got ta drink?"

"We have beer, whiskey, water, sarsaparilla, coffee, and milk," the waiter answered.

"I'd drink a beer iffen it's cool. If you ain't got none o' that then I guess I'll have some boiled water, cooled," Earl Ray ordered.

"Yes Sir...very good Sir, coming right up," the waiter said as he turned and walked away.

Earl Ray looked around at the dining room and wondered how many years the hotel had been there in Kissimmee. The walls were tongue and groove lumber nailed vertically on the sides of the room. The doors and windows were placed so the sun would not shine in, yet the breeze that would be caught up into the dining room and keep it relatively cool in the Florida climate. The large windows ran from the floor to the eleven foot ceiling, with screens on the windows and screen doors on the entrances of the café. The white walls were a dingy gray caused by smoke from the kerosene lamps, also from the many hours of candles burning, so people could see to read the menu and eat their meal.

In a few minutes the waiter brought Earl Ray a large mug of cold beer. Then asked "Are you ready to order now?"

"Yep, I guess I am; kin I have a steak like I had last night? With gravy, boiled taters, and let me try some of that sweet corn, too. Oh yeah, and pea can pie and a cup of coffee," Earl Ray ordered, as he thought that would be about the best he could order since he couldn't read the menu.

After his dinner, Earl Ray strode back onto the wooden sidewalk, took out his new Barlow folding knife, and cut a long splinter off the pine column supporting the over hang of the café. He used the splinter as a toothpick and then wondered what he was going to do with his spare time. Accustomed to always working, riding or tending scrub cows, he felt a little uncomfortable and perhaps bored with this new lifestyle he was now sporting.

Remembering Jeremiah Coxin, Earl Ray wondered what he was doing about now. He found himself standing in front of the livery stable. As he peered in, his old horse neighed and snorted. That's when Earl Ray decided to leave this big city life in Kissimmee and go hunt up Jeremiah at Fort Blount.

He had his horse saddled and paid the livery man what he owed. Then he rode the horse to the hotel, got down, and hitched the horse to the railing. He told the man that he would pay for the room and then leave. The clerk told him that if he was leaving, he would not charge him for that day. Earl Ray went up to his room, packed his old trail clothes in saddlebags, strapped on his Colt, picked up his Winchester, and went downstairs.

As Earl Ray walked out of the hotel, he almost bumped into a portly, but pretty lady who was walking toward the general store. For a moment Earl Ray stepped aside, then he recognized the lady. She was the lady from Bent Penny Cow pens, Mr. Allbritton's housekeeper.

Earl Ray doffed his new Stetson hat and spoke to the lady, "Scuse me, Ma'am. Ain't choo the lady from Bent Penny Cow Pens?" Ain't choo the lady what's at Mr. Allbritton's house?"

The lady looked startled and answered, "Yes, I am. Why do you ask?"

"Well…Ma'am…I'm…er…Earl Ray Remmick. I been one o' the cowboys what Mr. Allbritton bought our'n cows two weeks ago from. And I'm really happy to see you agin, so's I kin thank you agin. I ain't forgot how good you fed ole Jeremiah and me. Yessum, yore cookin spoiled me for trail grub, don cha know, and special your pea can pie," Earl Ray stammered like a school boy trying to talk to a girl he liked and didn't know what to say or how to act.

The lady blushed and started to turn and walk away.

Earl Ray gathered up all the strength he could muster and took her by the arm. She straight away linked her arm inside his, and they ambled to the general store together.

Inside Bodow's general store, Mr. Bodow greeted them and asked how he could help.

"Mrs. Sykes, it's such a pleasure to see you again. I hope that Mr. Allbritton is well. If he is in town, he had better not leave without saying hello and maybe even playing a game or two of chess with me. Now please, Mrs. Sykes, let me help you with your order," Mr. Bodow almost pled. He took the list from the lady's hand, read it, then looked at her and said, "It will take me the better part of an hour. Would you two like to look around while I fill this order, or have you other things which you need to do while in town?"

The lady responded, "Yes I do have to talk to Mrs. Petty down the street. She's sewing a dress for me to wear to the dance next Friday night."

Earl Ray thought, "I never knew what her name was and never thought to ask her. I wonder if she would like to have coffee and pie with me at the café? I'll ask her when we leave the store."

"Very well, Mrs. Sykes, you just come back in about an hour. I'll have it ready for you," Mr. Bodow said.

Mary Sykes turned to leave the store but first took Earl Ray's arm again. Nonchalantly, they stepped out into the sunlight.

Earl Ray cleared his throat and asked, "After you finish at the sewing lady's shop, could we go to the café and have a cup of coffee or sumpin lack that there?"

Mrs. Sykes looked at Earl Ray and saw a boyish look on his face. Then, she smiled and said, "Yes, let's do just that. I could use a cup of coffee or tea about now. I haven't had anything to eat since three thirty this morning before I left Bent Penny, and now it's almost four o'clock."

The visit to the dressmaker was short. As she came out of the shop, Earl Ray was there waiting for her. They linked arms again and walked across the dusty street to the café.

It was cooler in the café now because the sun was on the back of the building, and the pleasant odors from the kitchen were a treat within themselves.

Earl Ray thought, "It's funny that I ain't smelt that smell afore. The cook must be making a really good supper, I hope Mrs. Sykes will eat some of it, too."

They sat at the same table where Earl Ray had eaten dinner. Also, the same waiter came and spoke to Mrs. Sykes, then turned to Earl Ray and said, "You want another steak like at dinner time?"

Earl Ray flushed and said, "We would lack some coffee, then we'uns will thank about iffen we wonts to eat supper now."

The waiter brought a steaming pot of coffee and two cups and saucers, placed the items on the table, then left.

"May I pour your coffee…Mister…er…ah…Please forgive me, I have forgotten your name, and I am embarrassed that I have done that." She stammered, almost tearful.

"Ah...Earl Ray...Earl Ray...Earl Ray Remmick, Ma'am. Don't be 'barrassed none about that cause I didn't know whut yore name was till I heered it at the store, Mrs. Sykes. And yess'um, iffen you will. And would you like some pea can pie or some cake? They's baked em fresh this day," Earl Ray said, finally gathering his wits about him.

They talked small talk as they sipped the coffee, and Earl Ray found out that Mrs. Sykes' husband was killed in the War Between the States. Now, she was smiling and enjoying the special treatment she was getting from Earl Ray. Suddenly she noticed the time.

"Oh my goodness, look at the time! It will be midnight or later when I get back to Bent Penny," Mrs. Sykes said with an air of panic in her words. "Well I guess I could stay the night at Mrs. Wampler's boarding house and return in the morning."

"Why don't choo stay rat cheer at the hotel the night?" Earl Ray asked then added, "I'll be glad to pay for you a room. Will you do that? Then we can just eat supper here to the café and talk sum 'ore. I shore would lack that iffen you'll just stay. I ain't got nothing else to do till daylight when I'm gonna go see iffen I kin fine Jeremiah out to Ft. Blount. I'll see at choo git to home safe, don cha know."

"Well, I don't know. I usually stay over at Mrs. Wampler's boarding house when I'm in town late," Mrs. Sykes told Earl Ray. She added, "I haven't any sleeping clothes either."

Earl Ray said, "Why don't choo go to the general store and get whut yore gonna need to stay the night, and I'll pay for that, too."

"Well I don't know if I should..." her voice trailed off as Earl Ray interrupted her. "I ain't got nothin but respect fer you Ma'am; and I hope that you ain't took nothin from my invite here to the hotel. Why, I hope you a took no fence to what I said. You see, I ain't never enjoyed no woman lack I have enjoyed you this day. You know jist a talking and a listenin to what we talk about, don cha know." Earl Ray spoke the words with real humility in his voice and added, "Is it alright what I said? I respect you as the proper lady which you have been."

The purchases were made at the general store including a night gown, robe, slippers, and some toiletries. The packages were to be delivered to the hotel room which Earl Ray had gotten for Mrs. Sykes for the night.

They loaded the wagon. Then, Earl Ray drove the wagon to the livery stable and had the livery man unhitch the wagon and take care of the mules for the night, along with his horse.

The couple met again at the café and ate supper. Then, they sat and visited again until the waiter said that they were closing for the night. Well, it was eight o'clock anyway and time for the cracker cowboy to go to bed. Saying goodnight to Mrs. Sykes was somehow painful to Earl Ray as he had never felt the strange feeling in his stomach that he was feeling now.

The smell of coffee and bacon cooking awoke Earl Ray, luring him to the café next door. He started to dress in his trail clothes but thought he would rather be seen sporting Mrs. Sykes in his new duds.

Soon he was downstairs and sitting at his table when Mrs. Sykes entered the café. She was dressed in a new frock and had a bonnet in tow.

The waiter assisted Mrs. Sykes with her chair as Earl Ray just stared at her. It was as if he was seeing her again for the first time. It was apparent that Earl Ray Remmick was smitten by this portly lady from the cow camp.

The wagon was hitched as daylight began to break into dawn. Driving the wagon to the hotel, he found Mrs. Sykes waiting on the wooden sidewalk.

"Are you ready to go Mrs. Sykes?" Earl Ray asked as he climbed down from the wagon.

"Do we have everything?" Mrs. Sykes asked Earl Ray.

"Yes'um, and iffen you don't mind, I'll tie my ole hoss to the back wagon stake and drive you ta Bent Penny," Earl Ray suggested.

Soon they were following the ruts southwest toward Lake Wailes. Having about thirty miles to travel, they chatted as they went along.

"Mr. Remmick, may I call you Earl Ray? And if you will, please call me Mary," Mrs. Sykes asked after about an hour's travel.

"Yes'um and I thank that Mary is about the purtiest name there are fer a lady," he replied.

Now, as the ruts of sand led into the scrub, Earl Ray thought about his Colt pistol hanging over his saddle and the Winchester riffle in the saddle scabbard. Then he thought, "Oh well, I don't think I'll need them."

They stopped at a small spring near a hammock for a rest and to water the horse and mules. The animals nibbled on the fresh grass while Earl Ray made a campfire for some coffee.

Mary took some bread and cheese, which they had bought at the general store, and laid it out on the tailgate of the wagon.

With the coffee done and ready to drink, Earl Ray brought the coffee pot to the wagon. As he turned around, he almost dropped the coffee pot. The surprise was so great that his heart jumped, too.

On the edge of the hammock, just thirty feet from their camp, stood three Seminole Indians. They had come up to the camp without a sound and were watching the two people.

"Good gawd! Where did them injuns come from?" Earl Ray asked nervously.

"I don't know; I didn't hear them either," Mary spoke quietly, then offered them some bread and cheese.

"Don't feed them cow stealin injuns. Iffin I can git to my gun, we won't be bothered by them heathen red skinned rustlers. Besides, them fellers will wont them supplies, too," Earl Ray almost shouted.

Mary said, "I don't think so. You see, I know these Indians from a long time back." Then she said, "Hello Chief Billy Bow Legs. Welcome to our camp. Come now and eat. Have some coffee with us. I want you to meet a new friend, Mr. Earl Ray Remmick. Mr. Earl Ray Remmick, this is the high Chief Billy Bow Legs."

"They usually camp on the creek between Fort Meade and Star settlement but they sometimes come out to Bent Penny and camp while they hunt. Mr. Allbritton gives them a few of his cows and marks them for the tribe. He always sends his hands with the herd to make sure that they are not rustled by ruthless cracker cowboys," Mary told Earl Ray.

The Indians walked over to the tailgate of the wagon as Mary cut large slices of cheese and served everyone a slice. After asking if they wanted coffee, there were three silent nods. From the supplies in the wagon, she pulled out three more tin cups.

"Got sweet for coffee?" Billy Bow Legs asked.

Dutifully, Mary opened the cloth bag which held ten pounds of sugar and gave the chief a spoon. He took eight or ten heaping spoonfuls of sugar and stirred the coffee. Raising the tin cup of steaming hot coffee to his lips, Earl Ray thought, "This is gonna be a sight when that Indian sticks that hot cup to his lips." The chief drank the coffee and did not flinch. Earl Ray's mouth dropped open as he could not believe what he had just witnessed. "Why, that coffee was scalding hot; and that Indian just drank it down."

Following suit, the other two Indians sweetened their coffee just as the chief had, then started to drink. They were not as immune to the hot cup as the chief was, however, and both immediately set the cups down rubbing their burned lips.

The chief, Mary, and Earl Ray roared with laughter, for it had indeed burned the chief's lips. However, he would not let the others see him in pain because he loved pulling practical jokes on his braves.

Mary took the lard bucket out and had the Indians smear some on their lips to soothe the burns. They promptly licked the lard off their lips, so Mary told the chief to let it stay as it would stop the blistering perhaps.

"Lick good. I like," the chief told Mary. "Give more to take?" he asked, so Mary put some in a piece of oil paper and wrapped it up in a red bandana for the chief.

They ate the cheese and bread, finished the sweet coffee, then asked for sugar to take with them. Giving the chief the rest of the bag of sugar, Mary inquired, "Chief Bow Legs are you going to stay here or will you ride with us for a few miles?"

The chief answered, "We ride, too."

After packing up the remaining supplies, Earl Ray hitched the mules to the wagon, tied his horse to the stake, boosted Mary up on the wagon seat, and then climbed up beside her. He cracked his whip which caused the mules to bolt the wagon out of its deep ruts, and then pull together as the wagon groaned into motion.

The sun was getting low in the west when the wagon, with its company of Seminoles in tow, came into the clearing at Bent Penny Cow Pens.

Mr. Allbritton met the group as they pulled up to the porch of the house. Earl Ray climbed down and helped Mary from the wagon to the porch. It seemed that he held onto her waist a bit longer than necessary as Mr. Allbritton observed and wondered why Earl Ray showed up with Mary. Instead of inquiring, he turned and greeted the Indians, "Welcome, my friend Chief Billy Bow Legs. You are welcome to my home. Won't you come in and sit at my table? We will have supper on in a few minutes."

He held the door open as Mary walked in, followed by Earl Ray and the Indians. Mr. Allbritton closed the screen door behind him, as he saw to it that the chief was seated first. Mary went immediately to the kitchen and started supper. While the supper was getting done, she changed into her house dress and apron. Next, she set the table with the china that Earl Ray recognized from the trip before, which helped him feel more at home now.

After the meal, Mr. Allbritton offered each man a cigar which was accepted by the Indians causing them to exit to the porch to enjoy the evening and a good cigar.

Noticing that Earl Ray had lingered at the table with Mary, Mr. Allbritton withheld any remarks except side glances at Earl Ray as he went to the porch. It was not his custom to question any of Mary's relationships, although Earl Ray was the first that Mr. Allbritton knew anything about. At least she did bring him home with her instead of sneaking around behind his back.

Sometime later, Mr. Allbritton came back to discover Mary reading to Earl Ray from a book of poetry. He couldn't tell which Earl Ray was enthralled over: the poetry or Mary. Looking up from her reading, she asked Mr. Allbritton if he wanted anything.

"No…no…thank you Mary, I'll just sit here and listen to you read if you all don't mind," Mr. Allbritton answered.

Mary responded, "Not at all, I'll only read a few more pages, then I must turn in for the night. It has been a long day, Sir."

Earl Ray spoke up, "Mr. Allbritton, would hit be all right iffen I sleep over yonder in the hay barn? Soze I can git up and go soon in the morning and head for Fort Blount?"

Mr. Allbritton genuinely replied, "I wouldn't think of you sleeping in the barn when we have a nice guest room for you to stay the night. So you just get your trappings and spend the night here in the house with us."

Then he added, "The Indians are camping down by the creek and will be leaving before sun up. You and Mary can have a few more minutes together. I think I'll turn in now if Mary isn't going to read any more to us."

Mary blushed and said, "Please, Mr. Allbritton, sit down and let me finish this poem. Then we will all call it a night."

Earl Ray awoke to the delicious aroma of bacon and coffee cooking in the kitchen. Hurriedly dressing in his trail duds, he rushed to the kitchen to find Mary busily starting her day at Bent Penny Cow Pens.

Finishing breakfast, Earl Ray borrowed a lantern and went to the stable to saddle his horse. The stable was filled with the aroma of sweet nettle hay, and his old horse had eaten a fill of it. Not being accustomed to so much of a different kind of food than scrub grass, the horse was bloated and very flatulent. Going through the motions of saddling his horse, Earl Ray noticed it not breathing right. Taking the saddle and bridle off he started for the house when he almost ran face-to-face into one of the Seminoles.

With an armful of twigs and leaves, the Indian headed straight to Earl Ray's horse and began feeding the herbs to the horse. Next, he turned to Earl Ray and gave him the sign to stay here for another day and night. After that, the Indian led the horse to the water trough where she drank long and deep. For very obvious reasons the horse was left tied outside. Sure enough, the next morning, the horse was well and raring to go.

Sincerely thanking Mr. Allbritton, Earl Ray offered to pay him for the two days and nights he was there. However, Mr. Allbritton took offence to the suggestion of payment.

"Why, if I wanted pay, you would see a for rent sign on the door. The very idea of me taking money from a guest really galls me," he ranted. "Now, if you come back this way in a week or two, I want to talk over some business with you and with Jeremiah, too, if you can get him here." Mr. Allbritton shook his hand and said, "Don't forget to say good-bye to Mary also."

"No sir, I ain't gonna forget to do that cause she's been a mighty special lady. I cain't go lessen I tells her good-bye," Earl Ray admitted.

"Well, good-bye, Mary. Ah'm gonna be back here in about a week er two. So don't fergit me, and I shore won't fergit you neither," Earl Ray stammered. Then, going out to the barn and saddling up his horse, he turned to lead the horse from the stable. There stood Mary in the glow of the lantern looking like an angel to Earl Ray.

Boldly, she walked over to Earl Ray. Placing her hands on his face, she tenderly kissed him. Embarrassed, but surprised, he pulled her into his arms and ardently returned the kiss. Mary breathlessly whispered, "I couldn't let you get away without telling you that you are the most caring man I have ever known. You're so special to me. If you never come around me again, I just wanted you to leave knowing this: I have never been interested in another man since my husband, certainly never been in love. The other day in Kissimmee when I met you again, I knew that I was falling in love with you. Now that you know how I feel, I do so desperately hope to see you again."

Earl Ray pulled her close to him again and passionately kissed her, knowing that she would definitely be seeing him again.

Not ever wanting to release her, he softly promised, "I'm gonna be back here in one week now, and I'm gonna brang Jeremiah with me. So you have one o' them there pea can pies cooked and ready for me an Jeremiah." With one last hug, he reluctantly pulled himself away and departed. He couldn't wait to get back.

The trip to Fort Blount took a day and a half. Finally when Earl Ray led his horse into the livery stable, he noticed that Jeremiah's horse wasn't in the stalls. Wandering over to the general store, he asked if anyone knew where Jeremiah Coxin was. The man behind the counter said that he had bought some supplies and was heading to Tampa to see how the stockyards were run.

Earl Ray thought, "If he wants us to run a stockyard, we had better learn to read and count."

Finding the boarding house where Jeremiah was staying, Earl Ray asked if he could rent a room, too. The landlady told him that Jeremiah's room was paid for and if he wanted to, he could stay there until Jeremiah came back. Thankfully, he took the room and settled in.

Two more days of the week he had promised Mary to return were gone and now he was getting anxious to get back to her. That afternoon Jeremiah finally came riding up, tied his horse to the post in front of the boarding house, and entered. He was pleasantly surprised to see Earl Ray there in the parlor.

Greeting Jeremiah, Earl Ray told him enthusiastically about Mary. He also explained that Mr. Allbritton wanted to talk business with them, that they had to leave right now for them to get to Bent Penny Cow Pens within the promised week.

Jeremiah said, "Well this here is sumpen else. I was a gonna leave this evening to find you to see iffen you want to go into business you an me?"

Earl Ray answered, "Shore. Now let's git t'gitten over ta Bent Penny."

The pair arrived at noon at the end of the week and were greeted at the door by Mary and Mr. Allbritton.

Remembering his last visit to this stable, Earl Ray took the horses in. As he fed and rubbed them down, Mary appeared in the doorway. Meeting halfway, they embraced and kissed with a passion they had never felt before. Gently releasing each other, they strolled arm-in-arm to the house together.

Seeing their warm glow, Mr. Allbritton broke out a jug of corn whiskey and poured a shot for Earl Ray and Mary, as they sat down at the table to eat supper.

The talk at supper was mostly small talk about the price of cattle at the Tampa stockyards and the estimate of how many cows the scrub would yield this spring.

After supper, Mr. Allbritton filled their shot glasses again and offered the two guests a cigar. As they smoked the cigar and sipped the whiskey, Mr. Allbritton began to speak.

"You boys know I'm almost eighty years old, and I'm really tired of this cattle business. I'm going to make you all an offer which I hope you will not refuse. I have checked you boys out and I find that you are honest and have moral character. I am pleased to find two young men that are so incorruptible, for I want to make you this offer.

For a lifetime interest in the business, I will sell you the complete trade here which consists of two hundred forty acres and the option of the entire section and township. It is mostly scrub, hammocks and palm islands. The best land that is clear enough is here at the Bent Penny Cow Pens.

Now, I propose that I sell you the land, business, and my good will for ten dollars on the condition that you can't remove me from this site for the rest of my natural life. I have asked Mary Sykes to write all of this down. If you will sign it, I will start my retirement tomorrow."

Shocked, Jeremiah spoke first, "You mean yore gonna give us me an Earl Ray this business fer ten dollars? What are we gonna do with this here business?"

Earl Ray was speechless.

Jeremiah continued, "Me an Earl Ray here cain't even read reading or write writin. How we gonna run a business?"

Mr. Allbritton said, "Look, all you have to do is pool the money I paid you for your cattle. When spring comes, there will be enough money to buy the cows the crackers bring in here." He then added, "You can do what I did to start out: buying as many cows as you have money for, then agree to pay the crackers for the rest when you get back from taking the herd to Tampa.

Usually I buy the cows for ten to twelve dollars a head. Then, if the cows throw calves, that is more profit for you. You take the total round up to the Tampa stockyard and sell them for twenty to thirty dollars a head. That more than doubles your first year's investment which allows you to buy more cows the following year. Just remember to keep enough cash on hand to pay the cowboys if they want cash instead of a bank draft"

Jeremiah spoke up, "Yeah, ah been gone to Tampa. Them stockyards was a payin thirty-four dollar a head this past week. They was a shippin em to a place called Cuber and some of them was a goin to the government to feed the soldiers some beef. So a bunch of them cow critters was a goin on a steamboat to New York."

Coming out of his shock, Earl Ray questioned Mr. Allbritton, "How many head did you drive to Tampa this time?"

"With the cows you boys brought in, I drove twenty thousand head to the stockyards this summer," Mr. Allbritton replied.

"Wheew!" Earl Ray whistled. "At there shore is a heap o' cows, and I cain't even think of that much money."

"I banked five hundred and twenty thousand dollars. And that is more than enough to see me through the rest of my life. But remember, when I die, that money will go to Mary Sykes, the hands, and you two boys. And Earl Ray if you will get busy and marry her, she will be a good business manager for you," Mr. Allbritton chuckled.

As they hesitated, Mr. Allbritton added, "Do you want to think about this deal overnight? Jeremiah looked at Earl Ray, and they nodded to each other.

"We'uns don't need ta thank it over. We want to do it. Did you say that it is writ on paper, Mr. Allbritton?" Jeremiah asked.

"Yessir…Mary will you hand me that contract please?" Mr. Allbritton requested. Mary passed him the papers and pointed to the place where Jeremiah and Earl Ray were to sign or put their mark.

Earl Ray spoke to Mary, "Will you walk outside with me before I sign this here paper?"

Mary arose from her chair while responding, "Of course. Come on we'll walk out to the cow pens."

The moon was full, and the autumn evening was pleasant for Florida weather. They walked to the rail fence, and Earl Ray put his foot upon the bottom rail. Tenderly, he looked at Mary for a long moment. Cicadas serenaded from the old oak trees.

"Mary, I ain't good at saying wots in my heart, so I'm gonna just plain ast ye if you will marry me before I mark that there paper? I want to be sure that you will stay with me and help me to larn t' reading, write writin, and to count and cipher so ah kin know what them cowboys is a got commin to them when we buy them cow critters from em." Earl Ray had actually proposed, and he felt as though he were ten feet tall. Now he patiently waited for a reply from Mary.

"Yes, Earl Ray Remmick, I'll marry you; and now, we are promised to each other. So you go ahead and sign that contract and I will always be your wife and helpmate for the rest of our lives." Accepting his proposal, she smiled warmly at him, making him feel on fire inside. Taking her into his arms, he passionately sealed the proposal with an embrace and kiss.

The deal was made. The crackers in the scrub were now businessmen, and Mr. Allbritton gave Mary away at the wedding. Jeremiah was Earl Ray's best man.

The married couple happily settled into the cabin which the hands had hastily built for them while they were away on their honeymoon at the hotel in Kissimmee. The cabin had a wooden floor and a pump and sink in the kitchen. There was a single bedroom and a living room opening to a front porch. The porch had a swing and was often in use in the evening.

Each morning, Mary arose early and headed to the main house to cook breakfast for Mr. Allbritton, Jeremiah, Earl Ray, and all the hands. However, Mary had a Negro lady, Willie Mae Luke, to help her. She was the wife of one of the hands and lived in a cabin on the house property.

Mr. Allbritton was all astir one particular morning as he went about his work of the day. Earl Ray noticed his nervous activity and finally asked, "Mr. Allbritton whut got a burr under yore saddle? You dun wont to hurry everything up so. Whut's got in t'ya any how?"

Mr. Allbritton remarked, "Well if you really need to know I am going to take a trip to see some old friends in Savannah, Georgia. I'm going to catch the train at Fort Cummins and then the steamboat from Jacksonville, to Savannah. I'll be gone about three weeks, but I'll be back in time to help with the round up."

The day came for Mr. Allbritton to leave on his trip, and all the hands came to bid him farewell. John Henry Luke drove up in the buggy and loaded the bags in the boot and strapped them in. Mr. Allbritton stepped in and waved good-bye to all, then shook hands with Jeremiah and Earl Ray. "You boys stay busy and be good to each other. I'll see you in three weeks."

John Henry cracked the whip, and the buggy leapt forward through the gate where it soon disappeared in the scrub. Mr. Allbritton was on his way for the first vacation he had ever had.

A strange, dark, vacant feeling enveloped the old house and office as though the spirit of the place followed Mr. Allbritton down the lane.

Mary shivered and Earl Ray, patting her on the shoulder, said, "It do seem a might lonelier without Mr. Allbritton, don it?"

"It's just that I've never been in this house when he wasn't in it, too. I guess that old man has grown into my life so that it feels like a part of me has been cut off." Mary seemed to sigh the words as Earl Ray and Jeremiah both nodded agreement.

CHAPTER FOUR

THE SCRUB BANDITS

Earl Ray and Mary's bedroom was next to the office. The window to the office was closed, and a stick propped the sash. Suddenly, in the stillness of the night, came the sound of glass breaking.

Startled, Earl Ray jumped out of bed and eased over to the bedroom door. He heard footsteps inside the office and the sound of someone trying to pry open the roll top desk. Picking up his Colt pistol, Earl Ray eased out through the door. Making the sound of a frog croaking, he heard one in return. He was relieved to know that Jeremiah was awake and had heard the commotion of the breaking window pane. The two tiptoed to the door of the office, then listened. The old desk was giving way to the prying of the roll top.

Motioning Earl Ray to stay in place, Jeremiah snuck outside and around the back to the office window. Turning the corner, he spotted another figure standing outside the window. Quietly easing up behind the man, Jeremiah lifted his Colt and clubbed the figure over the head. Blood spattered from under the stranger's hat as he sank to the ground, unconscious from the blow.

Not knowing what had happened, Earl Ray turned the doorknob to the office. With a loud clatter, the other man inside dove for the window saying, "I got it. I got it!" As he started out the window, the Colt pistol found that man's head. From the blow, he didn't get all the way through the window, slumping half in and half out.

"I guess that's been the both of em," Jeremiah said.

Just at that moment, a shot rang out from the scrub just behind the house. The bullet hit the window facing just in front of Jeremiah's nose. Splinters of glass flew and stuck into his face. He shouted to Earl Ray, "I saw the flash! You stay put and keep me covered!"

Jeremiah dropped to his knees, then cocked the pistol. He heard a horse running toward the house. As soon he could make out the silhouette of the horse and rider, he fired the pistol. The horse dropped and threw the man spread eagle into the yard in front of him. As the horse got up and walked away, Jeremiah sighed and was glad he hadn't shot the horse.

Earl Ray came out of the house with a lantern and held it over the man laying there face down. Turning the man over and seeing that his bullet had creased the head just over the eyebrow with blood spurting, Jeremiah used the man's bandana to wrap his head. Next, he got a lead rope from the barn to tie him up.

Earl Ray had taken time to check the other two men who also had not moved and cursed, "Dang it, Jeremiah, you must of hit this un mighty hard. He ain't breathing no more." Then he turned to see if the man who was hanging out the window, was alive. To himself he mumbled, "Feller, you gonna have one big headache in the morning," and finished pulling him through the window onto the ground beside the man that Jeremiah had shot.

During the time that Jeremiah and Earl Ray were busy with the three robbers, Mary took up a position by the front door with the Winchester. As soon as she saw that she wasn't needed, she headed to the kitchen and put on the coffee pot.

In the meantime, the hands, having heard the ruckus, had armed themselves and were rushing up to the house.

The others wanted to hang the three men right away, but Jeremiah objected, "No, you men just look at em whilst me and Earl Ray get dressed." Then he added, Mary is making coffee and ah thank y'all kin eat breakfast kinda early this morning."

"Tom, you and Cliff saddle up yore horses and see kin y'all find the other horses. We need to see iffen they's got brands or marks,," Earl Ray ordered two of the men, "Then you can take them to Fort Blount to see if'n the sheriff knows who they be."

At daylight, one of the robbers gained consciousness and began moaning and crying from the excruciating pain in his head. When one of the hands said, "You best enjoy that there head a poundin cuz Mr. Jeremiah could of put one of them forty-five bullets in it jest as good as club you with that Colt pistol."

The other man who fell outside the window sighed, moaned, then passed away. No one seemed to care. The hands lined up to examine the three would-be robbers to see if they could identify them. They each denied any recollection of having seen the men before this and went on to work.

Tom and Cliff had hitched up the wagon, put the dead men in, and threw a canvas over them. Then, they put the wounded man on the tailgate, tied his hands, and bound him to the body stake.

"Have the sheriff send after them fellers' horses and gun rigs iffen he wants em. Meantime, I'll keep em. If some of the hands need a gun, these uns 'll be fer em to take," Jeremiah told Tom and Cliff. He gave them twenty dollars for travel money and sent them on to Fort Blount.

Five days later, Tom and Cliff returned to the cow pens and went directly to the office to tell Jeremiah and Earl Ray what the sheriff had said.

"Y'all got some dead or alive money fer them fellers," Tom told his bosses. "The sheriff said that them fellers was wanted by the army and most of the state of Flar'dy." Then he added, "What them fellers is a been a doin wuz stealin horses from the army and the other ranches in Flar'dy. How come they was here was cuz they heard Mr. Allbritton telling his friend that he had sold the trade to y'all. I recon they wanted to get yore'ns money."

Proudly handing Early Ray a bank draft for five thousand dollars, Tom also turned over twelve dollars of the travel money to Jeremiah. "We spent some money to feed and livery the team. The sheriff put us up at the boarding house so that didn't cost nothing, and we et mighty good, too! Ceptin it weren't goodern your cookin Miz Mary."

Jeremiah handed the balance of the travel money back to Tom and ordered, "You and Cliff divvy this money up. That's fer doing a good and honest job for us. And we be thankin ya on top o' that."

CHAPTER FIVE

THE PANTHER

The weather was cold, and the wind gusting enough to make the Star settlement brisk. The freezing wind pierced through the cracker cowboys.

Even the horses snorted their displeasure of the icy wind they breathed into their nostrils. Snorting and lowering their heads did nothing to keep the frigid air out of their noses.

Shivering, Earl Ray endeavored to keep warm by clapping his hands together and rubbing them through the gloves he wore. Nothing helped. He thought of stopping and building a fire just to get warm again. To make matters worse, the dark, low clouds had rolled in again, threatening rain.

All of a sudden, Earl Ray's horse halted. Absolutely nothing Earl Ray tried would make her move another step.

"Dagumit, you old bag of bones, you better get going, or we both will freeze," Earl Ray shouted at his horse over the howling wind. "What in the sam hill are you waiting for? A warm barn?" Frustratingly, he added, "You ain't got the sense God promised a brass billy goat." Now git a movin, you ole nag."

But she would not budge from that spot even though Earl Ray tried to spur her on. Up ahead, Jeremiah's horse was still walking; but he turned the mount around to face Earl Ray and called out, "What choo thinks wrong with her, Earl Ray?"

"I ain't got a notion," Earl Ray responded as he stepped down and patted the horse on the neck.

All at once, there came a scream from the woods in front of them, just off the trail. Then another scream sounded ending with a low growl.

Frightened, both horses reared and neighed simultaneously. A scream came once again; however, this time it was at the very edge of the woods, just in front of the two horses.

Swiftly, Jeremiah and Earl Ray wheeled their horses around to try to get some distance from the screams.

"At's a painter there in them woods, and I cain't see where he's at neither," worriedly announced Jeremiah. Then he excitedly commanded, "Earl Ray, you best git back in the saddle cause iffen that there painter was to spring, you'll be higher and might git him with a pistol shot."

They both promptly drew their pistols and turned their mounts head to tail so that each of them could watch the other's back and any movement from the flank.

Listening intently, they couldn't hear anything but the wind blowing through the pines and palmettos. The loud whipped sound of the palmettos moving in the wind made it even more difficult to hear anything coming through the scrub.

"*YOWEREEEEE,*" wailed another scream. Even closer, it came from a large, low-hanging oak tree.

Unable to see the animal, the horses nervously pranced in a tight circle and angrily snorted. Their ears were back, their eyes displayed a look of terror. Suddenly, Jeremiah and Earl Ray spotted the yellow coat of the panther as it sprang to a lower limb of the tree, then disappeared back into the scrub.

"Jeremiah, let's go back to the west fork and see if we can come around that critter," Earl Ray yelled, as he spurred his horse back to the north. Filled with adrenalin, the horse had no trouble moving now. As Jeremiah was brining up the rear, the painter shrieked again. "Now, he's in the front of us again, ain't he," Earl Ray proclaimed.

"No…no, Earl Ray. I think it's either two or three of them painters. One got behind us, while we were watchin fer them at the front," Jeremiah said.

There was a sudden rush in the palmetto bush to Jeremiah's right. Then, quick as lightning can strike, the panther sprang onto the back of his horse, scratching and biting Jeremiah in the shoulder. Aiming at the panther's chest with his colt pistol, he fired his first shot. The panther went limp and slid from the back of the horse.

The fear of the panther, plus the smell of the blood from the deep claw marks and scratches on its rump caused the horse to frantically rear and buck. Still stunned from the commotion, Jeremiah was thrown from his horse right into the palmetto bush on his left. The palmetto cut into his face and arms. In shock, Jeremiah felt his shoulder to see if it was bleeding badly.

Reaching for his Colt, he cocked the hammer, in order to be ready for another shot. Stealthily, another panther swiftly approached from behind him.

"Shoot him, Earl Ray, shoot him!" Jeremiah yelled. But it was too late. This panther pounced onto his leg and fiercely bit into his calf. Painfully, he felt the bone grind between the cat's teeth.

Jeremiah was unaware that the third panther had tried to swing onto Earl Ray's horse just as Earl Ray expertly drew back his whip and cut the panther's midsection. While the panther began licking his wound, Earl Ray struck him again, this time putting out an eye. Quickly, the panther lunged at him, and the whip found its mark again, this time finishing a gash in the stomach of the cat. Lying down on the cold sand, the panther started eating its own intestines. At this point, Earl Ray aimed his Colt and dispatched the second panther. Turning, he saw that Jeremiah was in trouble and realized that he shouldn't shoot the panther that was attacking. Instead, he again expertly cracked his whip, hitting that cat in the rear end.

As the cat jerked around to see what had bitten him, Jeremiah accurately fired his Colt into the back of the third panther's head.

On the ground, three panthers lay, each at least six feet long from tip of nose to tip of the tail.

The horses were calming back down as Jeremiah tried to stand. Wincing in pain, he collapsed back onto the ground.

"Hey, Earl Ray, come and help me git up off the ground. I think I broke my lag, and I'm bleedin purty bad, too." Jeremiah whined to Earl Ray, who was already off his horse and frantically rushing toward Jeremiah.

First, he tied his neckerchief around Jeremiah's leg wound then stripped Jeremiah's coat off to see how badly he was bleeding. Finding only puncture wounds gave Earl Ray relief; however, there were many bites that had found their way through his clothing. The fact that it was cold and he had on extra clothing probably had protected him from having serious injuries to his shoulder. His leg was a different matter. The panther had bitten an artery which was now spurting a lot of blood from Jeremiah's calf.

Quickly, Earl Ray found a small stick and started twisting the 'kerchief' to make a ligature to put pressure on the others to stop the loss of blood.

With the wounds protected now, Earl Ray helped Jeremiah back into the saddle. Carefully, they started to ride on toward the Star settlement which was about five miles ahead.

In a slow trot, it took a little more than an hour to reach the settlement and shelter.

Immediately, Earl Ray took Jeremiah to the general store to see if anyone was capable to treat Jeremiah's wounds. The owner of the store promptly helped bring Jeremiah into the store and sent one of his sons to fetch the doctor.

Carefully, they laid Jeremiah on a small cot. To make it easier for the doctor, Earl Ray took off Jeremiah's clothes and covered him with a blanket.

No doctor arrived; however, an old woman who was a midwife came to the rescue. By that time, Jeremiah was dangerously weak from the loss of blood.

The lady had brought several poultices which she placed on each puncture wound, then turned to the store owner asking if he had any broth she could feed to Jeremiah. The owner brought some broth as well as some hot tea.

Putting her hand directly on the bleeding wound, the woman held her hand in place for about twenty or thirty minutes. When she released the pressure, the bleeding had stopped.

"Now don't you move a twitch. If you do, you gonna bleed again," the lady warned as she began feeding him the broth and hot tea.

Afterwards, Earl Ray went outside to find shelter for the horses at the livery stable along side the blacksmith's shop. He knocked on the door, but no one answered. Opening the door, he led the two horses inside, unsaddled them, and pitched them some hay. He searched until he found some pine gum salve and doctored Jeremiah's horse where the panther had dug his claws into the rump of the animal. Last, he brushed them quickly and went back to the store to check on Jeremiah, who was now fast asleep.

While Jeremiah was recovering, Earl Ray went to the Star settlement to meet some crackers and discuss the round up in the spring. Many of the men were eager to talk and listened intently to Earl Ray tell about the plan set forth by Mr. Allbritton. After lots of discussion, only one of them declined to sell his cows on the "come and wait" until the cows were taken to Tampa and sold to the buyers there. After that, Jeremiah and Earl Ray would return with the cash to settle up with the cracker cowboys.

Earl Ray offered to give the cowboys a contract which he and Jeremiah would keep until they returned from the round up and trail drive to Tampa. However, most of the cowboys told Earl Ray that there was no paper that was any better than the handshake of an honest man.

Earl Ray agreed to pay cash to the hold out. Finishing his business there, he went back to the general store where Jeremiah was. He asked the lady how long before Jeremiah could be moved?

Well, if he ain't a good friend, you can take him now. Course he'll die before you git to the scrub. And if he's a good friend and you want him to get well, you best let him stay right on that cot for three weeks," she said.

"Three weeks? I guess I'm gonna hafta leave him here and let you tend to him. I'll take his horse home with me tomorrow though," Earl Ray stated.

Heading out, Earl Ray noticed the freeze had begun to kill the moss in the oaks. Even the oak leaves were turning black and falling. There was ice on the ponds. Even in the cypress swamps, the water was frozen. Several times Earl Ray had to chop holes in the ice for the horses to drink, as he returned alone to the Bent Penny Cow Pens.

Eagerly meeting him at the door, Mary asked where Jeremiah was. Earl Ray told her the story, and displayed the skins which they had claimed from the three cats. Mary felt sorry for Jeremiah and the fact that he couldn't return home yet.

"I'll hitch up the wagon team and go get him in three weeks. I shore hope he'll be all right and won't have no problems later on from them painter bites," Earl Ray exclaimed.

Finally, three weeks had elapsed. Earl Ray and John Henry Luke headed for the Star settlement to gather Jeremiah as snow was falling in central Florida. Another unusual freeze had begun.

To make the bitterly cold trip easier for Jeremiah, John Henry had fitted the bows and canvas top on the wagon. If necessary, they could sleep in the wagon at night to stave off the cold and frozen ground.

Because of the bizarre weather and Jeremiah's condition, the trip took over a week to go and come. But all-in-all, Jeremiah fared quite well. Under Mary's nursing, he was able to get up and about just one month after the panther attack. Lucky for him, he had suffered no permanent injury.

As a precautionary measure, Earl Ray went to Kissimmee and brought back two new twelve gauge shotguns. From then on, they were attached to the saddles of both men. If there were to be a next time, they weren't going to try to shoot any more panthers with a Colt pistol. But if they needed to shoot a longer distance, they'd have the Colt, too.

CHAPTER SIX

CRACKERS AT THE SALT LICK

Jeremiah Coxin had finally healed pretty well from the panther attack and was presently riding with David Crocket Pierce, the railroad surveyor, to find the boundaries of the township which had been sold to Earl Ray and him, along with the Bent Penny Cow Pens' business. They rode and camped for days while Davy and his crew surveyed the land.

Davy was now an independent surveyor and had become a civil engineer.

"A engineer?" questioned Earl Ray, "You done surveyed all them railroads and now how come you gotta run them trains on it?"

"Earl Ray, I'm not that kind of an engineer. I do the survey first. Then I can draw up and map out what I have surveyed," Davy chuckled.

"I know you musta learnt moren you never knowed afore then when we found you in the scrub that night," Earl Ray noted.

"I guess so, Earl Ray, but sometimes I wonder if I have learned what I really need to know," Davy spoke with a trailing-off sentence. He had just spied a new feature in the scrub, the likes of which he was unfamiliar.

"What's that strange looking clearing over there, this side of that cypress bay head?" Davy asked.

"Where bouts is it? I don't see anything different. I jist see them dead trees there. Looks like light ling kilt em. You want to go see bout em, Davy?" Jeremiah asked.

They rode the half mile to the edge of the dead trees, noting that there was a small spring in the center of the dead part of that forest.

Davy dismounted, walked over to the spring, squatted down, and stuck his finger into the center of the spring. Tasting the water coming out of the ground, he announced, "Salt, it's a new salt spring which has come up to the surface and is killing the flora in this little dip." He stood up and looked around the area, then added. "You all had best get the hands to come out here and cut down all these trees and clear this part of the glade. Then you'll have a salt lick for the cows. Also, dyke it up so it doesn't overflow into the swamp there," as he pointed to the northeast stand of cypress." It'll kill the whole swamp inside of a year."

Soon thereafter, Earl Ray brought Tom and Cliff to the area to explain to them what Davy had suggested to do about the salt lick. In addition, he recommended that they get enough men to get the job done soon because the dip was filling fast.

It took the hands about a week to clear the area of the salt spring. When completed, they noticed that every evening just before sundown all kinds of animals were coming to the salt spring to drink a little of the salt water. They observed deer, coyotes, raccoons, opossums, and even snakes.

Davy stated, "Maybe God has supplied the salt for the animals in this area since the only other salt I know of is up in the Pane's Prairie area. There's a salt marsh there where cows are often driven to get the benefit of the minerals."

Since the clearing was finished, the hands were presently building the berm around the dip to retain the salt water from seeping into the swamp. All at once, Chief Billy Bow Legs and his party appeared – seemingly out of nowhere.

"You find salt?" the chief asked.

Jeremiah replied, Yessir, it's a salt spring, and we's a dammin er up to keep it out of the swamp."

The chief took a stick and started to draw on the dirt. He made several squares, and each was joined by a line from one side of a square to the next square and so on for four squares. Then he looked at Jeremiah, then at Earl Ray and said, "You make dig like that from salt spring. Then water fill one that make full a more start fill. Make all fill. Stop water from spring. Let sun dry. Soon have much salt for animals all round. Make good medcin for cows, horses, and other deer and animal."

"By gosh!" Davy almost shouted, "You know what! The chief has shown us how to make salt pans. After the water evaporates or soaks in the ground, you can take rakes and rake up the salt to use, even in your home. I know the Indians will like the salt because they need it to help cure their meat for the winter. Why, this will possibly even be another enterprise for the Bent Penny business," Davy excitedly exclaimed about what the chief had shown them.

"Davy, do you want to know which a way that there'll work?" Jeremiah asked. "Cause iffen it's at easy, mebbe hit ought' a been yoren, you kin jist pay me n' Earl Ray in whatever salt you ain't sold yet."

Davy said, "You mean, you want me to run the salt business for you?"

Jeremiah said, "That's whut I thought I said at choo. Iffen it ain't plain, I reckon at's what I'm a sayin."

Davy explained that while the salt was drying, he could go on with his surveying and engineering. He still had a lot of ground to cover and map for the cracker cowboys.

That night, Jeremiah and Earl Ray talked it over with Mary and concluded that David was the right person to run the salt business. It was as he had said. The salt pans would take care of themselves.

Soon, however, they discovered that was far from the case. It was next to impossible to dry salt in the Florida climate. When the rains came, the salt was dissolved again, and the process had to start anew.

Davy consulted books on geology, but there had been almost no study done about salt pans, or about drying anything in Florida. He contacted several people whom he knew in Brunswick, Georgia to discuss the problem, but they had no experience concerning the drying of salt.

Eventually, the solution came from a mistake that Mary made in the kitchen when she was boiling saltwater to cook potatoes for supper. The pan boiled dry while she was preoccupied by another problem in the house. When she discovered her mistake, she started to throw the crusty white powder away. Instead, she set the pan aside and started another for the potatoes. When Davy came into the kitchen to ask her a question, he noticed the pan on the drain board and asked Mary what it was.

"I boiled the saltwater for the potatoes dry and had to start another pot to boil them in. I didn't want to take time to clean the pot before I used it again, so I took down another one. Why?" Mary asked.

"Well, young lady, I think you just showed me how to make the salt business work without having to depend on a Florida drought to dry the salt pans." Davy smiled as he spoke. "I was about to give it up as a bad deal I had made with the bosses, but now I have an answer to this problem."

Davy ordered his workers to build a large lean-to at the salt pans while he traveled to Kissimmee to get in touch with the turpentine people. He was looking for a large kettle like the one from the Lake Wailes still. But since it was now fall, most of the stills were shut down until the next spring when the sap would easily flow.

Just outside of town there was a crew grinding sugar cane. The large square pans were concentrating the cane juice into syrup. A new idea took over, and he asked the man, who was skimming the syrup, where he got the pans to cook the syrup in. The man told him to wait until evening when they were finished with the day's work. Then he would be happy to show him the catalog he had.

After a while, the brand new pans arrived with fire brick and steel to make the ovens at the cow pens. They were taken to the new shed which the hands had erected for them. Next, they were installed in clay brick ovens where a fire was kept going twenty-four hours a day until the water had all evaporated down. Then, more salt water was added until the brine was saturated with the salt. After that, there was a layer of salt about an inch thick on the bottom of the pans. Their first run netted them over one thousand pounds of salt, and it was the purest anyone had seen coming from an evaporation system like this one.

Their troubles were not over, however. When the salt was stored in a regular barn, it began to collect moisture in the cotton bags. When it dried again, it was rock hard.

To solve that problem, Davy built a barn with double walls and large cracks in the floor to aid circulation. The walls had straw with mud packed between them to insulate enough to prevent moisture from staying in the warehouse. Then, there was a small fire which was kept burning all the time. This was indeed the answer to the problem of keeping the salt from getting rock hard again.

Later, Davy discovered that if silicate was added to the salt water, when the salt was dry it stayed granular in the bags and did not hurt the flavor or integrity of the salt.

For Davy to make salt blocks to sell to the ranchers for salt licks for their cattle, the salt, which was processed without the silicate, was pressed into wooden molds and formed into twenty pound blocks. These were wrapped in oil paper and sold in most of the local general stores as well as some liveries.

Only about eighteen months after the new warehouse was built, Davy started realizing a profit on the salt business.

Every time the Seminole Indians came to the hammock, they were given several bags of salt a piece. Very soon, they were bringing smoked venison, turkey and fish to the Cow Pens to trade for salt.

Also, Jeremiah and Earl Ray always generously sent several hundred ponds of salt with the cowboys who drove cows to the Indian camp between Fort Meade and the Star settlement.

In addition, Mary added a hundred pound bag of sugar for the Chief Billy Bow Leg's coffee and several pounds of candy for the children. The children named her "Mama Sugar Candy," and they often sent her trinkets, which they had made. Mary sold some of the trinkets in town so that she could buy more candy to send the children for the next drove to the Indian camp.

CHAPTER SEVEN

CRACKERS AND THE DRY HOLE

The bat wing doors swung back and forth as Jeremiah Coxin and Earl Ray Remmick walked through them into the dark, stale-smelling saloon. They sauntered up to the bar and looked into the mirror behind various bottles. It was smoky and cracked. There was a bullet hole in the upper right hand corner of the gilded frame. Perhaps the errant projectile was meant for the torso of an unfortunate fellow cracker cowboy.

But that story ends there, as Earl Ray was wondering about the bullet hole and its reason for getting into the gold mirror frame.

"What'll it be gents?" the bartender asked.

"You got a cold beer?" Jeremiah asked.

"I got the coldest beer in Kissimmee. You want a five center?" the bartender asked as he drew two mugs of beer and sat them before each man.

Jeremiah took a long drink from the cool beverage and asked the bartender, "D'ya know a feller by the name of Scott Scofield?" He watched the bartender and the mirror to see what was happening behind him.

Earl Ray half turned to better scan the dark saloon and nudged Jeremiah as a man in the corner of the room slid his chair back and started to stand. Then, Earl Ray stepped toward the door. With the bright sun at his back, he watched the man easing toward the steps that led up to the second floor.

This man had a special rig with two colts and a fancy, tooled-leather belt supporting the two silver guns. The bullet loops each had a bullet, and they lined up from holster to holster. In the center of his back was a skinning knife that tilted at an angle in order to make it easier and faster to draw.

As the man started up the stairs, Earl Ray followed him with his eyes and watched him as he turned to look at Jeremiah's back. As he started to draw the Colt from the right hand holster, Earl Ray drew, hastily cocked his Colt, stepped to the side, and aimed.

Seeing that Earl Ray was deadly serious, the man let the pistol fall back into its holster.

"Whut's on yore mind feller? You got too twitchy fer me, and I thank you ought ta jist step down and ease over here. I ain't got much truck with no back shooters," Earl Ray drawled.

The man stepped over with his back to Jeremiah and faced Earl Ray. His hand moved toward the Colt again, but this time Jeremiah has his Colt out and stuck it into the back of the man. Next, he removed both pistols and the knife from the man's belt.

When the man felt the difference in weight of his gun belt plus the barrel of Jeremiah's pistol in his back, he let his arms relax and fall to his side. There was no way he could fight or flee from these two cowboys.

"Whut's yore name, Mister?" Earl ray asked.

"I'm Tobias Skinner," the man answered.

Jeremiah looked at the bartender, and the bartender nodded his head at the truth of the man's statement.

"Whut made you so twitchy you had to try to shoot Jeremiah here in the back?" Earl Ray asked the man.

"I had a notion you're bounty hunters a-lookin fer Scot Schofield. So I was gonna make sure y'all didn't git him," Tobias answered.

"You know where we kin git in touch with Mr. Schofield?" Jeremiah asked.

"Sure, he been up yonder in the room asleep. Him and me want to git back home from offen the round up. The better part of this summer we been kickin cows out of the scrub and driving them up ta Sanford," Tobias said.

"Whut's old Scot Schofield wanted fer?" Jeremiah asked.

"He been accused of stealin horse and cow critters. But he didn't do it. Him and me was in the scrub when them critters was stole. And now they got a two hundred and fifty dollar bounty on Scot's head. I ain't got none on me, cept mebby just ride'n with Scot." Tobias said defensively.

"All right, let's go and git Mr. Schofield out of his room. We want ta talk ta him and we ain't no bounty hunters. What we wont to talk about is buying his cows next year," Jeremiah said as he turned the man around and motioned for him to go up the stairs, "Whut room's he in?"

"The one at the head of the steps. He got purty drunk lass night, so he's probably still sleepin. And he do sleep like a log," Tobias said.

When Jeremiah and Earl Ray walked up to the room, to be careful, they made sure Tobias was in between them and let him open the door to the room which he said Scot Schofield was in. When the door opened, they saw a form lying still in the bed. The smell in the room was worse than an old outhouse. In spite of that, they entered the room and shook awake the man in the bed.

"Toby, if you don't go and leave me sleep, I'll jist whollop the tar out of ya," Scot warned.

"I ain't Tobias. I'm Jeremiah Coxin. Me an Earl Ray here done heered about yore round up, and we'd like to talk ta ya bout some business," Jeremiah spoke up. We gonna be downstairs awaitin cause it stinks so bad here. Earl Ray, git his Colt and gun belt, too, so he won't have no thoughts bout gittin nasty like Tobias done tried to."

The three went back downstairs and sat at a table to wait for Scot to come down. After about twenty minutes, Earl Ray said, "I reckon I'm gonna hafta go back and wake him good this time, cause we'uns need to git back to Bent Penny Cow Pens in a day er two."

Earl Ray climbed the stairs and went into the room, then came back out and announced that Scot was not in his room. He had gone out the window.

Jeremiah asked Tobias, "Where'd that feller go to?"

"I, uh, I don't rightly know cept mebbe to git hissen and my hosses cause I thank he thanks you been bounty hunters lookin fer his scalp." Tobias almost cried with the thought that Scot was up to something other than hunting cows.

The three men hurried outside toward the livery barn and stable. Suddenly, at full gallop, a horse and rider burst out of the stable, stepping aside, Earl Ray cracked his whip which startled the horse. Instantly, it reared and threw its rider to the ground.

"Now don't you try to git up and run, cause I kin crack a hoss fly from offen a hoss's rump 'n never make the critter flinch. Now git up, and let's go back ta the saloon so's we kin talk some business bout buyin your cow critters next year. And no more of yore funny stuff now neether," Earl Ray ordered.

Inside the saloon the bartender brought the unfinished beers to the table and asked if the other two men wanted anything.

Jeremiah ordered a glass of beer for each of them. When they had been served, Jeremiah and Earl Ray began to talk to the pair.

"Now I hain't never had so much trouble a tryin ta buy cows like I done had with you two. I done tole Toibias here, we ain't no bounty hunters. All we want ta do is make a deal fer yore cows next year. How many'd you git out of the scrub this round up?" Jeremiah asked.

Tobias looked at Scot. Then Scot said, "We come up with bout eight hundred head, but we lost better'n ninety head on the drive cause the water was give out along the way. Then we got to the swamp and two cow critters was gator got."

As they were talking, two more men walked into the saloon and up to the bar. They asked if the bartender knew a Mr. Scot Schofield. Motioning toward the four men at the table, the bartender replied, "The one with his back to the door is Scot Schofield."

The men turned and looked at the four men sitting at the table, then immediately left the saloon.

After Jeremiah and Earl Ray finished dealing with the cowboys, they walked out of the saloon. The morning sun was hot and the air was still. Most folks were inside trying to keep cool. The two partners walked their horses to the livery stable and gave them water. When the horses were finished, they mounted up and started to ride east out of town.

"Jeremiah, you gonna give them fellers their guns back?" Earl Ray asked.

Jeremiah said, "Yep, I'm a gonna give em ta the barkeep and let him sort them out."

Just then, two shots were fired inside the saloon. The two strangers who had inquired about Scot Schofield hurried out of the saloon. Another shot fired. This time it came from a shotgun, and one of the strangers fell into the street with a wound from the buckshot that hit his leg.

Earl Ray's whip once again found its mark and tore the pistol from the second man's hand.

The two men outside stopped in their tracks and were surprised that Jeremiah and Earl Ray were still around.

Earl Ray held his gun on the other two as the wounded man collapsed onto the boardwalk due to the loss of blood.

Simultaneously, Jeremiah went into the saloon where the bartender was bent over a person on the floor. It was Tobias. He had tried to shield Scot Schofield from the shooter's bullet and got hit in his right side. Scot Schofield was trying to help Tobias get up off the floor and into a chair, but Tobias motioned that he wanted to be left there.

A deputy sheriff came running into the saloon and looked at Tobias and Scott, then turned to Jeremiah and asked, "Did you shoot him?"

Jeremiah shook his head. Then the bartender spoke up, "Sammy, that there feller out there with the buck shot in his leg, shot the man on the floor. That's when I told him not to move cause them other two fellers had their guns. When I saw that feller shoot an unarmed man, I drew my shotgun. When they saw I had a gun, they shot at me, too. Missing me, they run out the door, but I nailed him with a load of buckshot when he wuz in the doorway."

To get the man on the floor some medical help, the deputy asked Jeremiah to go fetch the doctor from the café down the street. Then added, "I'll take care of the other two."

Having heard the shots, the doctor had already started into the saloon after stopping to look at the man on the boardwalk.

The deputy asked the doctor if he could move the wounded man who was outside. The doctor replied, "You can do whatever you want to. He's dead, bled to death… two or three of those buckshot hit an artery. I could have saved him if I had him on the operating table when he got shot. Now let's see if we can help this man."

Scot had already removed Tobias' shirt and opened his underwear to expose the round hole in his side.

"You're a lucky man." The doctor said, then turned to the bartender and said, "Albert bring me two double shots of whiskey."

The bartender got two glasses plus a bottle of whiskey, and then took them to the doctor. He poured one glass and handed it to the doctor who drank the liquid quickly and reached for the other glass as the bartender drew back. The doctor said, "Don't worry. This one goes to the wound, and the next goes into the patient."

They got Tobias up and over to the doctor's office where the doctor probed for the bullet. When he had extracted it he gave it to Scot and said, "Here you keep this. I hear it was meant for you anyhow."

"How come you had these men's guns?" the deputy asked Jeremiah.

"Well sir, we disarmed them fellers to keep them from shootin us. We had come back from waterin our hosses. When we got back to the saloon, the ruckus had done started. Earl Ray, here disarmed the other man with his cow whip," Jeremiah boasted.

The deputy said, "I have a wanted poster on the two men with a five hundred dollar bounty on them. So, I guess that Albert will get a bounty for the one he shot and that other man for capturing the other with his bullwhip."

Jeremiah replied, "Why don't you give hit ta Scot Schofield and Tobias, cause we been the ones that took them feller's guns away. We feel right bad about that now."

The deputy responded, "Well, suit yourselves. To make it legal, you'll have to sign the book fer the bounty money. Who you give it to or spend it on don't make no mind to me."

That afternoon Jeremiah and Earl Ray were riding east toward Saint Cloud to another ranch when Earl Ray spoke up and said, "Well, Jeremiah, we shore had a time with them fellers. Come to find out, them fellers that the barkeep shot was the ones what stole them cow and hoss critters: but them others got the blame. Then, we find out that Scot Schofield and Tobias is gonna quit bein scrub cowboys. I guess we could call that a dry hole."

Chapter Eight

MR. ALLBRITTON GOES TO TOWN

The steamboat River Queen with black smoke billowing from its twin stacks, edged gently toward the pier where she would berth for the night, then sail again before the sun rose the next morning. She was loaded with cattle, cotton, hog heads of tobacco, and passengers, who by now were scurrying toward the gang plank.

Mr. Allbritton was watching the docking through the porthole in the cabin he had called home for almost a week, since he had left Sanford, Florida. Now, the sight of Savannah, Georgia was indeed a great and welcome sight. Although weary of the travel, he was anxious to see his old friend from his brigade in the army of the United States of America. It was almost like Christmas or some other gay holiday from his past when he thought of seeing this friend of so many years. He wondered how his old pal had fared through the years since they had last seen each other when they had waved good-bye in the dusty clay street there in Savannah.

As the passengers slowly snaked their way down the gang plank and disappeared through the dark doors of the wharf, they reminded Mr. Allbritton of cattle being bunched up in the corral, they forced to merge into a single line to load or unload in cattle cars. The push was about to end, as he muttered to himself, "Well, look around one more time and see that you've not forgotten anything."

As he picked up his valise and duffle, there came a knock at his cabin door. He opened it and allowed the porter to take his baggage, then left the key to his cabin on the bedside table and closed the door behind him. He had to stoop in order to get his six foot frame through the cabin door without bumping his head on the top of the door frame as he had so often during the trip. When he stepped out onto the deck and into the fresh September air, he surveyed his surroundings.

Savannah had really come back to life after the war and now was a bustling city where trade was coming in and leaving by steamboat and by railroad. It was noisy too as he heard steamboat and train whistles, bells, and straw bosses shouting at the Negroes, who were at that minute rushing to get the boat unloaded from its trip up from the south. The Stars and Stripes were flying above the cupola of the terminal causing him to ponder the days when the Rebel battle flag had flown on that same flagstaff. It was compelling him to be thankful the war was over. And now, Savannah had recovered and become a wonderful Mecca for culture and trade here in the Deep South.

"John!....John…John Allbritton," came a shout from the railing on the dock. It was his old army buddy and lifelong friend, Wendell Hampton.

Wendell Hampton, was the same height and build as Mr. Allbritton but had noticeably aged more. His hair was totally white and blew in the breeze, as he waved his hat to get Mr. Allbritton's attention. Mr. Allbritton waved back when he had finally caught sight of Wendell in the crowd of people who had gathered to meet the River Queen.

Mr. Allbritton made his way down the now-deserted gang plank with the Negro porter in tow. Wendell led them through the terminal and back onto Bay street where his hansom cabriolet was waiting.

"Take us home, Dargon," he commanded his Negro driver, as the two friends stepped into the buggy. With his valise and duffel loaded into the boot, the driver cracked his whip guiding the matched team of mares into the line of wagons, carts, drays and buggies all plying for a lane of travel. Heading west through town, they travelled for thirty minutes before coming to a stop in front of a large brick, over-native stone house.

"This place is a mansion," Mr. Allbritton thought, "Wendell has done quite well for himself."

They climbed about twelve stairs to the stoop in front of the house, where a large black lady had already opened the door and was waiting for them to enter.

Mr. Allbritton whistled under his breath and said, "Wendell, you old coon dog, you got bigger than me. My place in Florida would likely fit into your hallway here." They laughed and Mr. Allbritton added, "'Cept I have a little more land where my home is than you have here."

Wendell remarked, "Yeah, but it ain't in downtown Savannah." They chuckled again as Wendell led them into the game room.

That room was a stark contrast to the bright and well lit entry of white Georgia marble with pink veins through it. The game room was dark and had many stuffed animal heads, mostly deer and antelope. There was a large bison head hanging just above their heads with a polished, brass plate beneath which read, "Remember me and the great hunting in Oklahoma." It was signed, Buffalo Bill Cody. Totally impressed, Mr. Allbritton told Wendell how much he enjoyed seeing the trophies.

Wendell poured them a shot of bourbon and toasted the renewal of their friendship and also to many fallen comrades from the war.

"Well, Wendell, what have you been up to? With all this, you must have really made some great strides of success since we saw each other last." Mr. Allbritton commented as he turned and sat down into a leather, overstuffed chair. Wendell took the chair next to him and said, "Yes, you know, I really got all this the old fashioned way... I married into it." This brought another round of laughter and another round of bourbon.

Soon afterwards, the large door to the game room opened, and a butler announced that dinner was served.

"Good," said Mr. Allbritton. "It'll be good to taste some good ole southern cooking again, and I am just about as hungry as a man can be and still talk about it."

The dining room was as ornate as the rest of the house with a large chandelier hanging in the center of the banquet room-sized table.

"I'm glad that Mary Sykes can't see this place. She would forget her station in life and want a house just like this one," Mr. Allbritton said,

"This sure is an elaborate home, and I certainly am looking forward to seeing the rest of this beautiful place of yours, Wendell," he added.

The dinner was a sumptuous meal of roast beef with pheasant, sea food, mustard greens, cornbread, rice and gravy. There were desserts which were rich and especially pleasing; however, the most surprising part of the dinner for Mr. Allbritton was the sweet iced tea. He had heard of the beverage, but in central Florida, ice lasted about as long as it would in hell. The sweetness of the drink was very delicious. In addition, a garnish consisting of sprigs of mint was hanging on the edge of the glass.

After the meal, the two men went back into the game room and talked until the wee hours of the morning. Finally, Mr. Allbritton looked at his watch and remarked, "Wendell, if we don't stop talking and go to bed, we'll run out of things to talk about; then I'll have to leave for home early."

The crowing of a rooster awoke Mr. Allbritton. After stretching a bit, he crawled out of the feather bed and stepped to the wash stand to splash his face. The cold water did the trick; it kicked the drowsiness out of his head enabling him to get dressed. After he was ready, he went downstairs and walked toward the game room where he thought he would write a letter to Mary Sykes Remmick which could be read to Earl Ray and Jeremiah. As he crossed the entryway a beautiful young lady, dressed in a riding habit was coming down the stairs.

"Good morning, Mr. Allbritton. I'm Brittany Hampton, Wendell Hampton's daughter. I'm very pleased to finally meet you. You have always been very highly bespoken of by my father, and we feel that you are a part of our family, too," she added, "Father, Mother, and I have already had coffee in the parlor. We were waiting for you to come down to have breakfast." And she led him to the patio where Wendell and his wife were sitting.

Wendell stood up and introduced Mr. Allbritton to his wife. "Mary Ellen this is..." She interrupted, "I know. You are John Allbritton. Wendell has spoken of you since we met before we were married. And I see you have met our daughter, Brittany. Please sit down and let's have some breakfast."

The breakfast was as delicious as the dinner had been the night before. And the Georgia smoked ham was about the most delectable food that he had ever eaten.

"I never have tasted a ham that was as delicious as this. I'll have to take some of this home with me. Mary and the boys will never believe how good this meat really is," Mr. Allbritton declared.

"Well you don't have to worry about that; we'll send you off with enough to keep you for awhile," Wendell said.

"I need to get one of your maids to brush and air my wool suit. It is now well traveled, since I could not air or brush it on the boat. It'll need a touch of pressing, too." Mr. Allbritton added.

"There's a Chinaman who has a laundry a few blocks northeast of here. We'll get your suit over to him and let him clean it up for you," Wendell disclosed.

"Good-bye Father. Good-bye Mother and Mr. Allbritton. I am going riding with a friend this morning, and I won't be back before dinner. So I'll eat supper with you all this evening. Bye for now," Brittany announced as she gracefully rushed from the patio and into the garden which led to the stables.

Becoming conscious of the time, Wendell announced, "Mary Ellen, John and I are going to the shop and office. We'll be back for dinner, then the three of us will go to the Savannah House for supper and on to the theatre to see the play that's billed there for tonight. I'll have Dargon go by and purchase the tickets while we're at the office."

While they were on their way, Dargon dropped the wool suit off and handed Mr. Allbritton the ticket from the laundry. Folding it, he placed it in his wallet as the buggy lurched forward toward its destination.

HOLT INDUSTRIES, the sign over the main entrance read.

"Holt Industries?" Mr. Allbritton asked, "Who is Holt?"

"He was Mary Ellen's father who started this business before the war and built it into a large foundry. He made castings for just about anything, so when the war started, he made cannon barrels and other castings for the war effort. He also made horseshoes from iron and even some rifle barrels. Ever since I met Mary Ellen, I had been working for him. When we got married, he made me a full partner.

61

Since his death, I'm totally in charge. Ironically, nowadays, we are now melting down cannon balls for the federal government since they are trying to get rid of all the old cannons and cannon balls in the arsenals around America. We got the bid to do the job for the southeast. However, major problems began when we tried to get the cannon balls open to get the gun powder out of them. At one time, we had thirty car loads of them, and we tried soaking them in water. That only made the powder more dangerous to work with. Drilling holes in them would cause the ball to get too hot which might cause an explosion and hurt or kill the pressman. Next, we dropped heavy steel weights on them which resulted in some of them exploding. Thankfully, no one was hurt however, the crane got knocked out. Do you know what we discovered the answer to be? Well, we took the lead plugs out of the balls, scraped what powder we could get out, and filled them with water. Finally, that winter when it froze the cannon balls would break open at the casting seams. Brittany actually is the one who solved the problem. That happened when she accidentally left her goldfish out in the cold. When it froze the fish bowl broke. Being heartbroken, she swore never to take another goldfish for a walk. After her period of grief, she had an idea that maybe freezing would do the same thing to the cannon balls. Sure enough, it did, and we have been doing that ever since.

The business also buys scrap iron and junk so that we can melt it down and use it in new castings. However, we had trouble with people stealing from the scrap at night when everyone had gone home. Finally, we hired a night watchman, but that didn't solve the problem because he slept most of the night. After that, we bought a really mean dog and would let him out after we locked up. He kept thieves at bay for awhile until some smart one thought of getting a bitch in heat and putting her over the fence with the watchdog. Well, he did what came natural, so when the dogs were hung up, the robbers went in and stole about a hundred dollars worth of scrap parts from the army.

What really made me mad is that I think we bought some of that scrap back from those fellows, so they got to me twice. Since we're smarter than thieves though, we had the dog castrated, making him meaner than ever. That is what took care of the stealing."

Mr. Allbritton was laughing hysterically at the oral picture which Wendell had painted about the junkyard dog and how colorful the story would be to tell when he got back home.

During his two weeks stay, Mr. Allbritton and Wendell went hunting, fishing, and generally took in the sights in and around Savannah. The most interesting part of the trip was the tour of the foundry to see how horseshoes were molded and hammered to the strength that was needed to wear the longest. Blacksmiths and horse-shoers, of course, had to fit the shoes to the hooves.

The time had flown by, and the time had come to return to Florida and home. Mr. Allbritton was a bit anxious to see the folks back home. As soon as the steamboat docked, he began supervising the loading of his gear, including four smoked hams, sausage, hog head cheese, cane syrup, canned vegetables and numerous other goods. These things had been lavished on him and dutifully packed in several barrels to protect the wares, while making the trip back to the Bent Penny Cow Pens and home.

After a long week aboard, the steamboat docked in Sanford, Florida where Mr. Allbritton found John Henry Luke waiting for him in the buggy. He informed John Henry that they would need to get a wagon to haul all the treasures home and also hire a teamster to drive the wagon to the Cow Pens.

Fortunately, the livery stable owner had a wagon and team that Mr. Allbritton purchased. Also, he was able to hire a man, named Billy Matson, to drive the wagon home.

After getting enough supplies for the trip to Bent Penny, the tiny caravan was finally on its way to central Florida.

In Florida, October is hot and humid, making their long trip very difficult to endure. The air smelled of rain, and the length of time would stretch even longer if they had to fight rainy, cold weather all the way. Ultimately, after eight days, the travelers reached the familiar clearing of the Bent Penny Cow Pens.

As usual, Mary was waiting on the porch, waving her handkerchief at their arrival. A group of hands who weren't busy at the time, also greeted Mr. Allbritton as he rode up. Mary explained, "Well, this is like Christmas with all the packages and food that you brought from

Savannah, Mr. Allbritton. How was the trip, and how did you find your friend."

"They were all fine. Wendell, like me, is getting older. I surely did enjoy the trip and meeting his wife, Mary Ellen, and his daughter, Brittany," Mr. Allbritton said with a bit of nostalgia in his voice.

"You reckon they'll come to visit us any time?" Mary inquired, "I sure would like to meet those folks. A person can't have too many friends, don't you know."

That night at supper, they feasted on Georgia smoked ham, along with grits and fig preserves on the biscuits. All the while, Mr. Allbritton spun all the yarns about the house, foundry, Wendell's family, and the junkyard dog. How comforting it was to be back home.

CHAPTER NINE

AMBUSHED IN THE SCRUB

The bullet hit the tree limb before the report from the rifle was heard. The next shot hit Earl Ray's Marsh Tacky in the head just above her eye. She dropped like a wet rag, and Earl Ray hit the ground, causing him to somersault. The next shot ricocheted from the cypress log, just behind the dazed cowboy.

Earl Ray yelled at Jeremiah, who was about fifty yards behind him and still out of sight in the scrub, "Stop whar you are! He done shot my tacky, and she's dead. You git down and slow. Watch whar them shots iz acomin from. I thank they want ta shoot from my right, west'o me, but a good ways out, cause I heered the shot after my hoss done been hit. And the limb from that turkey oak what he done shot first – it fell off afore I heered the gun far."

Jeremiah had already tied his horse to a sapling and was crouching in the palmettos when he heard horses coming down the dirt trail from the west like Earl Ray had said. He didn't answer Earl Ray but just hunkered down and waited.

Just as Earl Ray heard the horses, he bolted the few feet to his dead horse and grabbed his twelve gauge shotgun and his Winchester from their scabbards which were attached to the saddle. He had no time to get his saddlebag with his extra ammunition. While he was running, he vaulted over a cypress log and jacked a round into the Winchester. The double barrel shotgun was already loaded with double O buckshot. Then he waited.

The scrub was as quiet as a tomb, no birds singing, no rustling of the palmettos, just ear splitting silence.

Even though words were being whispered, Earl Ray couldn't make them out. Not making a move, he diligently listened for any sounds.

Suddenly, there was a noise as one of the bush whackers had tripped on a root and went sprawling, almost in front of the dead horse. As he angrily picked himself up and shook the white sand out of his gun, the other man appeared from behind a palmetto clump and said, "You got his hoss, so he cain't be far from here."

At that very moment, Earl Ray stood up and confronted them, while Jeremiah slipped behind them. His shotgun at the ready and his Colt tucked into his waist, Jeremiah was the first to say, "Don't move and y'all won't git shot!"

The two men turned in disbelief to hear Jeremiah behind them. One of the men dropped his gun and then started to reach for it. Earl Ray fired his Colt, and the bullet threw sand in the man's face. Immediately, they threw up their hands in surrender.

Earl Ray asked, "What choo reckon we'uns ought ta do with these fellers, Jeremiah?"

Jeremiah stepped up behind them and took their guns, "Well, I reckon they just need a hangin, and I'm jist ready to blige them right now, too," Jeremiah said smugly. Then he added, "Earl Ray, since they kilt your tacky, go on back and find where they done left their hosses at. I'll keep them covered." As he turned toward the two men, he commanded, "Now, you fellers lie down on your face cause I ain't fixin ta trust you'ens no how."

Just as the men got on the ground, as Jeremiah ordered, Earl Ray came back leading two horses and two pack mules. "They's got a herd back yonder a half mile. I thank they've been a rustling somebody's cows. We'll have to see the mark to know who them cow critters belong ta, "Earl Ray commented as he tied the two horses and mules. Motioning for Jeremiah to come to him, he lifted the canvas cover from one of the packs to reveal fresh cow hides, slated and ready for the tanning vat.

"How many you reckon is here?" Jeremiah asked.

"Looks lack a good many hides here. Let's look at the other'n and see whut's on that there mule pack," Earl Ray stated.

They threw the canvas back, and there were many more cow hides plus some deer hides, panther, raccoons, and other furs to be sold somewhere.

As they were tying the canvas back, a large skinning knife whirred past the cowboys. In a flash, they simultaneously turned and fired, striking the first man in the heart and gut. He fell dead to the ground while the other one fell over backwards.

"Earl Ray, git that there rope from offen that hoss and let's tie this feller up before he gits hurt or tries to hurt us," Jeremiah stated with urgency.

Quickly, they tied the man up and placed another rope around his neck so that it would have to be cut from his throat to get it off.

After that, Earl Ray and Jeremiah struggled to rescue the saddle from the dead horse, then put it on the thief's horse. Handing him his own saddle, Jeremiah stated, "Now iffen you want that there saddle, you gonna tote ht back ta Bent Penny Cow Pens."

"But that's five or six miles from here. I cain't tote that saddle that far. Besides, why cain't I ride that other hoss?" the man whined.

"You kin take it er you kin leave it, but I thank you will tote it iffen you knows whut's good fer ya," Jeremiah warned, then added, "You cain't ride no hoss. Them's all ourn now, and we ain't gonna let you ride. You gonna walk through this here white sand, and every step you take you gonna thank God that we didn't leave you hangin from that there turkey oak."

It was after sundown when they finally reached Bent Penny clearing. The two cowboys were met by Tom and Cliff while they tied the horses and mules in the barn.

Tom asked, "Earl Ray, where's the Marsh Tacky?"

"This here feller shot her in the head and kilt her. I got my saddle and bridle from offen er, but I didn't have no shovel to make this here bush whacker bury her. In the morning, me and this scoundrel is gonna go bury that ole hoss," Earl Ray explained.

Roughly, Tom and Cliff herded the prisoner into the tack room and tied the end of the rope which was around his neck to the rafter. They left just enough slack to allow him to sit on the floor; however, he could not lie down or move in any direction without choking himself.

When Mary heard the commotion, she rushed out to see what was happening. After seeing the man and hearing the story about the ambush, she went back into the house, shaken from the idea that Earl Ray could have been hurt or killed.

When the men came into the house for supper, Mary asked, "You gonna feed that feller out there in the tack room?"

Jeremiah and Earl Ray spoke at the same time, "No!" Then Jeremiah added, "He don't git nothing ta eat. He don't git no water, jist like he was dead."

"How's he gonna dig that there hole to bury your hoss iffen he ain't et?" Tom chided.

"He best figure that out hisself," Jeremiah answered.

The next morning, the man was untied from the rafter and led back to the site of the ambush, where the body of his dead partner was still lying. Strangely, no animal had bothered his body during the night.

"Humph, not even the varments bother this skunk," Earl Ray muttered with disgust. "Now dig and git my tacky buried."

Before the grave digger started, he asked, "You want me to bury Benjamin, too?"

"Naw, he can hist lay thar an rot. He's too sorry to bury, an I don't wont his likes in my ground," Earl Ray snarled.

The man started digging. About noon, when the sun was high overhead, he pleaded for water. Earl Ray reluctantly handed him a drink from the canteen that was on the pack mule and ordered him to keep on digging. About an hour later, the man had a hole large enough to bury the Marsh Tacky. To move her, a rope was tied around her neck, and the mule pulled the dead horse into the grave. After the hole was covered up, the man was again tied by the neck with his hands behind him. Then, they started back to the compound. It was dark by the time the thief was tethered again in the tack room.

"I need water and food. Please, Mister. Have mercy on me and let me eat an drink some water, please," the man pleaded as the door was shut and locked for the night.

About an hour later, he heard the tack room door being unlocked. At first all he could see was the lantern; then, he heard a woman's voice.

"I brought you some food and water. Even though you don't deserve it, I cain't let you starve. I wouldn't do that to an animal," It was Mary and she had fixed a plate of food and brought a canteen of water for the man to drink. "It's got salt in it so you won't go and have a stroke on me. After digging that hole for the horse, you must have sweated a lot, so you need the salt to keep your muscles from cramping,"

Mary spoon-fed the man instead of letting him loose to feed himself. He quickly gobbled the food and drank the water to the last drop. Then, he stood up and bowed politely to Mary and said, "Ma'am, I jist cain't thank you 'nough fer yer kindness. I don't deserve it lack y'all said. But I'm sure thankful you have such a big heart."

The next morning, it was Tom and Cliff who once again had to take a prisoner to Fort Blount to the local sheriff. Riding on their horses, they made the thief walk all the way. When they arrived, he was overjoyed to go into the jail cell where he could lie down for the first time in six nights.

It took Tom and Cliff almost five days to go and come from Fort Blount. This time, Cliff asked, "How much do you thank them fellers was worth ta the sheriff?"

Earl Ray answered, "I ain't got no idea. I jist know they was a rustling and skinning cows fer the hides. I wouldn't give ya a lead penny fer the both of them bush whackers and hoss killers."

"Well, I'll tell ya, they was worth seven hundred dollars each. Here she is," Cliff handed Earl Ray a leather money bag with seven hundred in gold doubloons. Earl Ray took the money bag, opened it, and looked in it, "Blood money. I jist as soon you hadn't brought this to me. I ain't got no feelin fer them fellers, but I shore don't lack ta git money fer killin a feller neither."

Mary took the gold and put it in the office safe, then entered it into the ledger as bounty money.

A month later, a deputy sheriff came to Bent Penny and handed Earl Ray, Jeremiah, Tom and cliff a subpoena to appear in court against the man they brought to justice.

The courtroom was hot; and the lawyers and judge, in their wool suits, were sweating and often wiping their faces and brows. The trial lasted about three days, and the jury found the man guilty to be hanged the next day.

After the trial, Earl Ray asked the judge what should be done about the stolen cows. They were in his cow pens to await the fate of the rustler. The judge ordered that the cows become the property of Bent Penny and be added to the round up and sold.

The four men took their time going back to Bent Penny. As a lark, they traveled by the spot where the first man was shot and left to decay on the ground. Oddly enough, the only thing left of the man was a skull with its grizzly grin now bleached white from the relentless Florida sun.

CHAPTER TEN

A BABE IN THE SCRUB

"Whut's that I hear over yonder, jist in the hammock? Hit sounds lack a panther a hollerin. I'm a gonna ease roun the edge jist to git a peek at whut it is we hear a hollerin." Earl Ray was cautious as he eased the horse around the thicket, stopping the horse every few feet to listen for any sound in the brush or palmettos. Nothing. Suddenly, he heard a muffled cry, and he listened for the growl at the end. There was none. Next, he heard what sounded like sobbing. Dismounting, he eased into the thicket.

"Jeremiah, hey, Jeremiah! You and Tom come over here whar I'm at. Come on now!" Earl Ray shouted. Immediately, he heard the hooves of the two horses racing to his spot in the scrub thicket.

"Whut is it, Earl Ray, that's got you so excited?" Jeremiah asked as he dismounted and walked to the spot where Earl Ray was looking down at the ground.

The spot was a patch of green scrub grass that grows like centipede grass. On the spot, lay an Indian woman who had just given birth to a healthy looking baby boy.

To haul the woman, Tom rode to the edge of the bay head. With his axe, he chopped down two cypress saplings about eighteen feet long. Next, he stripped the limbs, tied them with his lasso, and drug them to the spot where the woman and child were. Using their blankets and slicker, they formed a bed on the travois and placed the woman and baby on the drag. Tom slid the poles into his stirrups and used another branch for a spreader to prevent the drag from rubbing the horse's rump while pulling the hastily-built stretcher.

Tom said, "I'll go on to the house and let Mrs. Mary tend the woman and the child."

It took him the better part of an hour to get to the compound. When he rode up to the door with the travois, he called loudly for Mary.

Mary came quickly out of the kitchen door, wiping her hands on her apron. She saw the drag but had not seen the Indian and child.

"Who got hurt in the scrub?" She worriedly asked.

"None o' ourn folks, Miz Mary. Hit's a Injun woman. She had a baby in the scrub, but we ain't seen no sign o' Indians no where around." Tom talked to Mary as he lifted the baby from the arms of the Indian woman and gave him to Mary. Then, very carefully, he picked up the Indian and followed Mary into the house.

"Take her to mine and Earl Ray's room and put her on the bed. I'll put the baby beside her. Then you go and heat some water. I'll need it to bathe the child and the woman." Mary ordered.

Tom dutifully went to the kitchen and pumped another bucket of water and put it on the stove. He opened the fire box and put in a couple of pitch pine logs which would quickly make a hot fire.

The stove was roaring, and the water was about hot when Mary called out, "Tom, Tom, come in here quick! We've got a problem here."

Tom bolted into the room just as the Indian woman screamed and passed out. Her eyes rolled back, and she was not breathing.

"Whut's the matter, Miz. Mary? What happened to her? She ain't dead is she?" Tom asked excitedly.

"I don't know what happened, Tom. She just started to turn very ashen. Then you heard her scream when she passed out." Mary said as she raised the head of the woman and slapped her on the back.

The woman started breathing again, and Mary watched as the new mother began to nurse her baby.

Mary had taken off the woman's bloody clothes and piled them on a chair by the bedroom door. The woman was bleeding profusely, so Mary placed towels and more sheets under her to catch the blood.

As soon as the child started nursing, the bleeding stopped. Mary was amazed at the fact that there was no more blood.

Tom had taken a load of bloody towels and sheets to the wash shed for Mary and placed them in a tub of cold water, as Mary had directed. He took the poke stick and punched the bloody clothes into the water until all were wet and soaking. Then, he returned inside.

Mary had the new mother covered with a blanket and was in the kitchen making some broth for her.

The fed, washed and cleaned-up baby was fast asleep. In Seminole, the woman spoke to Mary. Sadly, Mary only understood a word or two. She pressed her finger to her lips in the sign for her not to talk, but to rest. Soon the woman was asleep and resting, as Mary slipped out of the room and into the kitchen to finish preparing the evening meal.

She turned to Tom and said, "Do you think you could find Chief Billy Bow Legs and get him to come here to the house?"

Tom answered, "I ain't sure, cept I'll ride over to whar I thank he's at, Miz. Mary." Immediately, he was out the door to where his horse was waiting. The travois had been removed from the horse and placed on the porch with the blankets and slickers.

To search for the Seminole, Tom rode in a wide circle toward Lake Wailes but saw no sign of the chief or his party. He rode until it was almost dark, and then headed back toward Bent Penny Cow Pens. This time, he took a more direct route which was almost on the edge of the swamp. Smelling smoke, he rode toward it. Soon the campfire and hunting party were in his sight.

As he rode toward the camp, he saw that the Indians were skinning several alligators they had hunted down in the swamp. One of the gators was more than ten feet long. His head was at least thirty inches long and would make a prize skin for the Indians to sell.

Chief Billy Bow Legs greeted Tom and asked how Mary was doing and if she needed anything.

Tom told him about the woman and baby they had found in the scrub and that she was at the cow pens with Mary. Then he requested that the chief go back with him to the house as soon as possible because Mary had sent for him.

Then the chief turned and spoke to the party. The Seminoles all nodded with a sort of grunt. Immediately, the chief mounted his horse and told Tom, "We go now."

They arrived at the cow pens long after dark. When they rode up to the house, Tom took the chief's horse and tied him to the rail fence at the corral while the chief approached the house and stepped into the kitchen without knocking.

Mary greeted him with a cup of coffee and watched as the chief dipped eight spoons of sugar into it and stirred. He had downed the whole cup in a very few swallows. As Mary refilled his cup, he asked, "You want to see me, bout woman and baby?"

"Yes, Chief. She's had a rough time of the birth, and we can't seem to talk to her or understand what she is saying. That's why I sent Tom out looking for you and your party," Mary explained.

"Me go look at woman; you come, too," the chief said and followed Mary into the room where the woman and baby were still sleeping. The chief walked to the side of the bed and gently shook the woman awake.

When she saw him, she gasped and tried to hide her face under the covers.

As the chief spoke to her, she slowly slid the cover back from her face and answered his questions.

Then he turned to Mary and explained, "She not have man. She got baby from white man, and he put her in scrub to die with her baby."

Mary's eyes filled with tears as she responded, "That's just awful. If we ever find that man, he'll pay for this and good." Mary was furious and wanted to horsewhip the man that would do this to any woman.

"Chief, will you take her to your camp when she can travel?" Mary asked. The chief shook his head and replied, "She not like other woman. She went with white. Now, she no can go to tribe. They will kill her and baby."

Mary gasped then asked, "If we keep her here, will the tribe leave her and the baby alone?"

The chief nodded, "You keep. She make good at cow pens. We make sure Indian not make bad things on her or baby."

The chief drank several more cups of sweet coffee, took a bag of sugar, which Mary had offered, and other items which the party could use. Before leaving, he asked about Mr. Allbritton and was told that he had gone to visit a friend but would soon return. Finally, the chief went to the humidor where the cigars were stored, took several, and put them with the other items Mary had packed for him.

The next morning, there were three large sacks on the porch filled with smoked gator, deer, turkey, and fish. The trove was taken to the smoke house and hung there for future meals of delicious smoked game meat.

Months passed since the woman and baby had arrived. Mr. Allbritton would often take the wagon and go to Fort Blount. One day, he returned home with a nanny goat and two kids. "The goat's milk will be good for the baby," he stated. Naturally, Tom was the one who was assigned to take care of the goat herd. Reluctantly, he did just that.

Tom would milk the goat twice a day leaving enough for the kids to suck. Growing fast, the kids were eating horse feed, hay and grass, so they didn't need as much of their mother's milk as before. With this additional nourishment, the Indian baby thrived, and its mother had more energy to help out. She was very well now and went about helping Mary in the kitchen. Awe struck to see what fine cooking vessels Mary had, and with great pride, she helped wash and scrub them until they were shiny as new. Learning to cook like Mary, she was eager to please everyone with her new found talent.

The baby was growing and was trying to sit up; however, his little bottom was still too round, so he could only sit while propped up with a pillow. He didn't cry very much, and the doctor had come from Fort Blount at Mr. Allbritton's request. The doctor found the child healthy and hardy, but there was a lot of concern from his mother because the doctor poked, prodded, listened, and thumped the child. Finally, he announced that the child was in very good condition.

The people at Bent Penny started seeing a change in Tom. It seemed he couldn't do enough for the Indian woman and baby. They would walk along the path and talk to each other in their own language. Somehow understanding what each was saying. Tom had started calling her Orange Blossom, a name she took to very well. And he was calling the boy, Billy, for his namesake was, of course, Chief Billy Bow Legs.

"You gonna marry that there Injun girl, Tom?" Earl Ray asked one day.

"Earl Ray, you jist hush up and don't make Tom fidget like he do when a body asks him that question," Jeremiah scolded, "You done got the bes woman in these here parts and now you gonna make Tom think he gotta have hisself a wife, too. Now jist you hush up about that," Jeremiah continued to admonish Earl Ray. Then they all laughed.

But not Tom. He looked at Mary and asked, "Do you think that Blossom would marry a old broke-down cowboy lack me?"

There came a hush over the dining room. All the men stopped eating and talking, intent to hear what advice Mary was going to give Tom.

Tom blushed as Blossom's eyes welled with tears because she understood what Tom had asked. Now she didn't know what the feeling was in the pit of her stomach. She lowered her head, and Mary said to all of them, "Now look. You've made Blossom blush." They all looked with sympathy at Blossom. From then on, that subject was not brought up again as public discussion.

After Blossom had been at the cow pens for a year, she was speaking good English because Mary had made an effort to teach her some new words every day. Now, when Tom rode up to the house, she would run to meet him. He would lovingly put his arm around her and accompany her back to the kitchen. She always poured a cup of coffee for him and would have just the right amount of sugar and cream for his taste. Also, she washed his clothes and trimmed his hair. One time when she tried to shave Tom, she accidently nicked him, causing him to bleed. From then on, she would not touch that straight razor except to place it in the protective box that was on the ledge in Tom's room. Often, they would go for evening walks if Tom didn't have the night watch; and they would stand at the corral and talk. One night as the moon was up and bright, they turned to walk back to the house and accidentally brushed against each other.

Without hesitation, Tom took her in his arms and kissed her for the first time. Blossom had been unaware of just how much Tom really cared for her until that moment. And she held the moment as long as she could.

Then Tom whispered, "Blossom I just cain't live without you. I love you, and I want for me an you to git married, if you'll have me."

Blossom answered with a kiss, and they held hands as they walked back to the house. Blossom disappeared into the kitchen, and Tom went to his cabin. He could hardly sleep because he kept thinking how much he loved Blossom. Also he worried about what a poor start they would have after they were married.

He awoke the next morning to the rooster's crow and started to walk to the door, when suddenly he stumbled over a body sleeping on the floor beside his bed. It was Blossom. She had slipped into his cabin, laid down beside his bed, and slept there the rest of the night. Putting Billy on a pallet near the fireplace had kept him asleep through the night, too. Tom told Blossom that it wasn't right for her to spend the night in his cabin until they were married. He explained that the hands would think the worst of them. From then on, she stayed in her own room; however, she still waited on Tom, hand and foot.

The wedding day finally arrived. Tom, Mary, Earl Ray, and Blossom had already been to Kissimmee to buy new clothes for the occasion. Tom had a new wool suit with a vest, a new shirt, tie, boots and hat. Blossom was outfitted in a white gown with a veil and train. She wondered at how much waste it was to have such a dress with so much cloth in it, but she was proud. Mary made sure she had all the right things for her wedding ensemble including a fancy garter for Tom to throw.

Tom was worried about how to pay for all the trapping which were being put upon the two betrothed. He was told over and over, however to just not worry about the money. Mr. Allbritton had paid for everything and the wedding, too.

The compound was decorated to the nines with crepe paper bows, wild flowers, and palms. The barbecue pit coals were cooking whole hog, and Cliff kept turning the hog over the coals. Plenty of beer, coffee, punch made from orange juice, and other fresh juices from the area were available. Someone even slipped in two jugs of homemade whiskey. Like a hawk, Mary guarded the punch bowl, fearing that the moonshine might find its way into the punch.

After the wedding, the bride and groom were whisked off to Kissimmee to catch a steamboat for a week-long honeymoon trip to Jacksonville.

Blossom wanted to take Billy with them, but Mary convincingly told her, "Blossom, sometimes you have to walk with your back to the wind, even when there is no breeze." Then she added, "Billy and I will make sure that everything runs okay while you are away."

Mr. Allbritton put an envelope into Tom's pocket and told him not to open it until they were on board the boat out on the river.

They arrived at the steam boat and were escorted to their cabin, which was away from the loud, gambling parlor. They could hear the steam engine working like a monster breathing. Soon however, they became accustomed to the loud noise and the constant sound was not keeping them from sleeping.

Often Blossom would stand at the rail and watch the landscape go by, marveling at the power of the boat to ply the Kissimmee River against the flow. By the time they had gotten to Saint John's River, Blossom was an old hand at finding her way around the boat. She and Tom would eat their meals in the salon, and then walk around the deck or go and watch the people gamble. In the parlor, they would look at magazines and books. Blossom was always astonished at the many things that were to be seen and experienced. She would only have these advantages because of Tom, who was her lord and master, and she loved it.

When Tom finally opened the envelope from Mr. Allbritton, he pulled out five one hundred dollar bills in cash plus a bank draft for another five hundred dollars. Another envelope was inside which contained a deed giving him two hundred and fifty acres of land in the northwest section of Bent Penny property. Speechless, Tom and Blossom dropped to their knees and began to thank God for all the good fortune which had befallen them.

When they returned from their honeymoon, Jeremiah and Earl Ray took them to their property. On arrival, they found that the land had already been cleared. A cabin faced a lake and had a long, sloping grade from the house to the lake. The lake was crystal clear and had a white sand bottom. Blossom could see fish swimming and minnows darting to keep from becoming larger fish's dinner. Overwhelmed with emotion, Blossom wept at the wonderful way she had been accepted into the Bent Penny Cow Pen's family. They were more than her friends. They were her very own family.

CHAPTER ELEVEN

CRACKERS IN THE RAIN

It had been raining now for four days, and there seemed to be no let up from the torrent. The gutters surrounding the house had done their task well, for the 500 gallon rain barrel was overflowing. The excess water, pouring down the sides, had created a circle of water and cut a small ditch as it meandered toward the creek. The creek was rising and had reached the edge of the clearing where the Bent Penny compound stood.

Mary Sykes Remmick stood on the porch waiting for John Henry to fetch another load of wood for the stove. As she watched the rain touch the ground, she listened to the drops hitting the shingle roof and then cascade down to the rain trough. There was little sound in the hammock. Occasionally a squirrel would chatter is disapproval with the soaking rain.

Willie Mae was in the kitchen humming a spiritual as she dug out a scoop of flour. The wet weather had caused the salt to turn into a solid block. Now the flour stuck to the one-pound scoop. She banged the scoop on the side of the wooden mixing bowl, then finished wiping the flour out with her hand. With her other hand, she grabbed a handful of lard and threw it into the bowl with the flour. Then she attacked the caked salt in the wooden salt box with the determination of a soldier, challenging an interloper. Getting a handful of salt was almost as much work as building the kitchen that she was cooking in.

"What on earth are you hammering on, Willie Mae?" Mary asked through the screen door. "I'm tryin ta git dis here salt loose 'nough to git a handful outen hit fer the bread, Miss Mary." She answered back, then kept on humming to herself. John Henry came up the porch steps, and Mary held the screen door open for him to carry in his armload of stove wood.

"Hit's bout time you got to gittin that thar far wood here. The far is jist bout gone out with you foolin roun outside in the rain," Willie Mae scolded John Henry, as he dropped the wood into the wood box at the end of the stove.

"Oh, woman, y'all gotta fussin ana naggin. Aint choo got nuthen in yore mouth cept scorn?"

"You two sound like I need to throw a bucket of rain water on you. It sounds like a cat a dog fight to me." Mary chimed into the fray then waited for either of the two to answer.

"Y'all sees dat, don't you, Miss Mary?" John Henry said as he headed out the door for another armload of fire wood.

"I swear, Miss Mary, you cain't live wid em, an ye cain't live wid outen em." Willie Mae said with a chuckle. "Why y'all reckon hits a rainin so much fer, Miss Mary? Are it a storm coming?" Willie Mae asked, then continued her humming.

"I'd say, since it's August that we could be in for a blow. But if this rain doesn't stop soon, we might ought to start thinking 'Ark'." Mary quipped, then added, "I wonder how a cypress ark would float?"

"Oh, Miss Mary, don't talk that way. Hit hain't't funny, and I don know bout John Henry, but I cain't swim a stroke." Willie Mae said with a quiver in her voice.

John Henry came back in with another armload of firewood and dropped it into the wood box also. Then he said, "Y'all needs mo far wood Miss Mary?"

"You better ask your boss," Mary Chuckled.

"I cain't axe my boss. He done been into the scrub a huntin she cows with calves," John Henry retorted, then looked at Willie Mae. She threw a dish towel at him and said. "If y'all don't git out of here, you gonna haft to wash the dishes."

John Henry dashed out the door saying, "That's woman's work, and I ain't got time no how."

Blossom had finished feeding little Billy and had laid him on a pallet to sleep. Then she came into the kitchen, washed her hands, and started helping Willie Mae knead the bread.

"If weuns cain't git this here kitchen warm and dry, this here bread ain't gonna rise a tall." Willie Mae told Blossom.

Blossom nodded and continued as Willie Mae started to hum again. John Henry came back to the screen door and announced, "I jist come from the well. Hit't full to even wid da ground. That mean we gonna be wadin water in a few hours iffen hit don quit a rainin."

Mary said, "I need to ask Mr. Allbritton what he does in such cases as this." Then she turned and went to the office where she had last seen him. Looking around, she was unable to find him anywhere in the house. She looked on the back porch to see if he had taken his slicker and old hat. They were indeed gone. Mary went back to the kitchen and started supper.

Mr. Allbritton, Jeremiah, Earl Ray, Cliff, Tom and John Henry were in the stable, standing in a circle, planning what to do if the rain did indeed continue.

Mr. Allbritton said, "If you want my advice, I would drive cattle to the ridge and let them graze there until the rain is over. Later we can round them up and head to Punta Rassa, or Fort Brook. If the army doesn't want any beef at Fort Brook, we can drive them on over to Tampa to ship to Cuba."

"Yessir, I like that idea, Mr. Allbritton, Sir," Jeremiah declared, turning toward Earl Ray.

"Sounds good to me," Earl Ray agreed.

"When you thank we oughta start the drive?" Tom asked.

"As soon as we can get the hands together and provisioned. We should plan on two weeks to either to get the cattle first to the 'Back bone' on top of the ridge and then another two weeks to either Punta Rassa or Tampa," Mr. Allbritton explained.

The supper bell rang, so the men walked quickly to the porch to wash up and get ready to sit down to eat. While they were eating, everyone heard the whip crack back in the scrub and also wheels of a wagon groaning through the thicket.

"Ain't none of our crew," Jeremiah informed them.

"Hit sound lack hits a needin a good greasing whut ere hit be," John Henry spoke up. "Y'all wants me to go see whut are, Mista Jeremiah?"

"Naw, let's eat. Iffen hit's comin this a way, then we kin see whut hit's bout." Jeremiah told John Henry.

They were finished eating supper when they heard the whip cracking out in the compound and a shout, "Hello in the house."

"At aire's David Crocket Pierce. He were a workin roun Tampa. I want to know whut he is a comin here fer," Earl Ray said as he arose and started for the door.

Davy and Will Henry came up on the porch. They took off their slickers, shook the rain off, and hung their slickers and hats on the pegs.

Earl Ray met them at the door, "Y'all git washed up and set down to supper. I know that David Crocket Pierce is hungry."

"Yes, Sir, I could eat a horse. But if you didn't cook a horse, I'll make do with whatever you got in the pot." Davy teased.

Mary and Willie Mae started putting hot food back on the table for their added guests. Davy then asked. "Would you have enough to feed the rest of the crew? They'll be here as soon as the oxcart can get here. We were surveying near the river east of Tampa, but the rains have swollen the river so that we had to knock off till the rain stops and the river settles back in its banks."

"That oxcart is whut's done all the squallin in the scrub?" Tom asked.

"Yes. We greased it only about two miles back, but the rain washed the grease out fast," Davy explained.

"How many men you got with you and Will Henry, Mista Davy?" Willie Mae asked as she started preparing for the extra people.

"There are six more coming, for a total of eight in all, Willie Mae." Davy answered.

Sometime later, the oxcart, with two large oxen pulling, ground into the compound. Then, the other men came up on horses and mules. Tom and Cliff helped the crew get the oxen, as well as the horses and mules, into the stable. They fed them hay and oats and wiped them down while they were eating. Next they went to the house to wash up for their supper. Getting out of the rain and into the dry warmth of the kitchen and dinning hall was a great relief to them.

After supper, they talked about flooding rains and questioned Davy about what the sailors were saying in Punta Rassa or Tampa. Was there a hurricane brewing, or was this just a summer rain that wouldn't stop? They also informed Davy of their plans to drive the cattle to the ridge until the rain ceased then on to the best market.

Davy and Old Will Henry said that the flood would keep them from Tampa for sometime and going to Punta Rassa was impossible because of the high water.

"We actually saw some houses floating away, so we know the water is deep in spots, too deep for cattle to swim. Also, the current is now flowing about six knots. Not many cows would make it in that current," Davy told the attentive men.

"With the high water and the flood, along with debris that is floating down the river, no ships are in ports. They are either riding it out at sea or have sailed to drier ports," Davy added.

Mr. Allbritton told the men that his plan would not work, and that they still needed to drive the cattle to the ridge out from Lake Wailes.

The oxcart was pulled under the shed, the axles greased, and other minor repairs accomplished.

After that, the provisions were loaded in the wagon. All the hands including the survey team's duffels were loaded in the oxcart.

The chuck wagon was amply supplied, and the mules hitched to it were ready to go. The yoke of oxen were in behind the chuck wagon, and the other three wagons were to let the hands sleep in to stay dry. When oil skins were tied to the oxcart, everything was ready to move out. Jeremiah ordered. "Okay, Earl Ray, let's move em out!"

Whips cracked and the gates were opened for the herd to start its trek to the southeast towards Lake Wailes.

After three more days, the rains finally subsided; and the sun came out with a vengeance. The heat was unbearable. The sun beat down on the wet soil, and steam started to rise almost immediately. Earl Ray said of the heat and humidity. "Hit done rain fer all that time. Now the sun gonna try to bile it all off in one day."

The mosquitoes, sand flies, deer flies, horseflies, yellow flies and snakes were the next menace of nature that were in abundance.

After that year of flooding, it took several years before there were again gopher tortoises plying the scrub. Most of them in the area had drowned due to the high water table and their holes filling with water.

Jeremiah and Earl Ray's herd grazed and rested in the central Florida highlands until the rivers were normal again, and the cattle could be driven to port in earnest.

That time came soon enough. Whips cracked to start the herd moving toward the western sunset, and the shipping port of Tampa.

Chapter Twelve

CRACKERS OUT IN THE COLD

The winter of 1895 was shaping up to become a record, with the coldest temperature recorded until this time. The sun had not shone for several days, as the cold front swept down from Canada. The cold rain began to turn to sleet, then gave way to snow flurries.

All of Florida was in the grip of the frigid weather that rushed into central Florida with a terrible howl of the wind as if to warn the people that there were bad times approaching and to take heed of the Siren of winter and her warning.

The fall season round up was complete, and twenty thousand and some odd, scrub cattle were herded into the surrounding pastures. This was the first phase of the fattening process for the thin, but agile, wild cows. The pastures used were rotated so that the grass could grow after each round up. There was never any hay to allow the cattle to subsist in case of short feed or drought which would take its toll on the growing and replenishing of the open range grass for the cows to graze.

As the mercury dipped, the cattle started feeling the freezing temperature. They began to low and bellow about their discomfort. And with the rain, they would move in close to each other for additional warmth. When the rain stopped for a while, steam would rise from the herd almost obscuring the view from the Bent Penny Cow Pen's clearing.

At three o'clock in the morning, Earl Ray and Jeremiah walked quickly to the bunk house and roused the men to start getting the cows moving around in the pastures.

Mary and Willie Mae had not slept but had stayed up while the men kept vigil over the dropping temperature. A bucket of water was placed on the porch of the north side of the main house. As the night grew colder, the ice in the bucket got thicker. When Jeremiah could no longer break the ice with his fist, he knew that it was time to wake the hands and get the cattle moving.

Mary and Willie Mae had breakfast and plenty of hot coffee ready for the cow hands as they came into the dining hall to eat and listen to the instructions from Jeremiah and Earl Ray.

The fireplace was roaring, and the oversized wood-burning cook stove was plenty hot. Yet, the hall was cold, and cypress plank walls seemed to be impervious to the north wind.

"Now, listen here y'all men. Hit's a gitten downright freezing out thar. An iffen y'all hain't got no heavy coat, then your time in the saddle will be only fifteen minutes. Then y'all git back to the house or the far, whichever one is the closest to you." Jeremiah almost had to shout over the wind howling outside the house.

"Y'all listen to what Mr. Allbritton has got to say, cuz he done been in a freeze a fore; an he done got a lot a know how. So hear him good. Hit might save your scrawny hides," Earl Ray warned the hands.

Mr. Allbritton stood up before the hands and started to speak. "Men, I don't recall ever having the temperature this low in Florida.

I'm guessing that outside right now is down below twenty degrees. Now with the wind blowing a gale out there, your skin will freeze in just a few minutes. So if you will take a kerchief or bandana and place it over your face, you will probably not get frost bite. If you need to, you can take a pillow case and cut eye holes in it to protect your face. Do whatever you need to do to keep your faces from wind burn and frost bite. Wear your gloves at all times. Do not take them off for more than a minute." He paused for a moment collecting his thoughts.

"What Jeremiah just told you about not being exposed to the wind for too long a spell is good advice. Heed it, and stay healthy. I will have the fires going here in the house, and John Henry will keep the stoves hot in the bunkhouse. Now we will have to work hard and pull together. And every four hours we will have food ready here in the house for you to come in and eat whether you are hungry or not. You will need a lot of hot food to keep you going in the cold weather." Mr. Allbritton turned and looked into the roaring fire.

"Oh, and one more thing, whoever is cutting the wood and toting wood will change off with one of the riders every four hours. We'll change over after each meal. Are there any questions?"

There were only murmurs throughout the hall, and most questions were asked by and to each other.

After the meal was finished, a few of the men went back to the bunkhouse and wrapped blankets around themselves. Some hastily put on extra socks and even wore two pairs of pants. Each of them had masks and replaced their straw hats with socks and towels looking like Arabs as they went to saddle up. They then paired off with a partner to keep a close eye on each other.

"Man, I moved from Kentucky down here to git outen cold weather," one man said as he climbed upon his horse and ducked his head to ride through the stable door and into the blustery morning.

The cattle didn't want to move around and seemed to be totally confused as to what to do about the crackers' demand on them to move and stir.

Newborn calves and their mothers were cut from the herd and driven to the stable to provide more protection from the elements. Yet, in some cases, the calf had already succumbed to the cold blast. The whips cracked, and the cattle lowed, moving very slowly to the command of the cowboys.

"We otter git some of this here cold in the summer. You cain't git these scrub cows to move, much less stampede any," Tom told Cliff as they rode around the bunched herd and then tried to move their horses through the center of the herd. But that was impossible. They were packed so tightly that if one cow fell over, the entire herd would, too.

The two just kept riding around the bunch, getting a cow to move every now and then, but with a lot of difficulty.

"Whew! We gotta go to the house and get warm. They cain't git a camp far to goin in this here wind," Cliff told Tom. They rode to the stable and tied their horses.

With the cows and calves coming in, the stable was getting crowded. They walked out and latched the door behind them.

Mary, Willie Mae, and Blossom had cooked smoked ham, bacon, and biscuits. There was honey, fresh butter, and hot cakes on the table. Gallons of hot coffee and lots of sugar to build calories in the crackers were ready, also.

Night was coming on, and the weather was getting colder by the hour. Soon the cowboys would really start to feel the tiredness of the hard day's work and the inclement weather. Already, Earl Ray had to wake two or three of the crackers up as they had dozed while sitting in the saddle.

"Go to the house, git you some hot by the far," he told them. "Then git some vittles," he ordered. "But whatever you do stay awake, you hear?" Earl Ray admonished the nodding crackers.

Jeremiah had gone to the tack room and retrieved a demijohn of corn whiskey. As each man came into the hall, he was given a shot of it. There was not a man who asked for a second because they could feel the warming effect even before they sat down at the table to eat.

Mr. Allbritton told Jeremiah and Earl Ray that they had best get some rest for four hours, then the next group of hands could be relieved to rest.

They were told to go eat, then go to bed. Each man obediently complied.

"I bet you hit's the first time them fellers went to the bunk house and went right to sleep cuz I ain't got no worry there's gonna be no poker games," Earl Ray told Mary as he slipped into his bed beside her. She had already put two more quilts on the bed to warm him up faster.

Instantly, Mary heard the regular breathing of the exhausted Earl Ray as he slept.

During the night, the men heard what sounded like rifle shots, as the bark on the trees burst. The sap had frozen and expanded beyond the ability of the tree to withstand pressure from inside the bark.

Except for the rest period, the sound of axes and saws was constant, as the men tried to keep ahead of the hungry fires in their houses.

Soon, tree limbs started to break from the weight of the ice on them. They would plummet to the ground, and, at times, barely miss a sawyer. The limb would be quickly chopped into the proper length for the stove or fireplace and loaded onto the skid sled to be taken to the wood pile.

At times, John Henry even had to take an axe to break the ice which was holding the stacked wood together. He had to keep a roaring fire going or the wet, cold wood would not dry fast enough to keep the fire hot. He was stacking more and more in the main house and the bunk house for it to thaw and dry out.

When it was time for John Henry and Willie Mae to sleep, they placed their pallets near the fireplace on the floor and watched over Tom's wife and the baby as they slept.

Blossom, Mary, and Willie Mae were working in shifts in the kitchen now, and the dish washing was seriously behind. When Mary came into the kitchen from her rest, she found Blossom dutifully washing dishes and boiling more water to continue the chore. Soon both Willie Mae and John Henry were washing, drying, and stacking clean dishes for the next go round.

As daylight began to break, enabling the hands to see, they went to survey the cattle. Fortunately, most had survived the night; however, those that had frozen were covered with almost an inch thick layer of ice.

Riding to check on the cattle revealed another problem. The horses were slipping on the ice because their iron horseshoes had little traction on the sheet of ice standing in the pastures. Therefore, cautious riding was required, as horses often slid a little.

The blessing of the day finally came when the sun peeped over the horizon. At last, the hands felt that the worst was over for the crackers out in the cold there at Bent Penny Cow Pens.

Chapter Thirteen

CRACKERS AND THE TEXAS TICK

Earl Ray looked at Jeremiah and asked, "Ain't hit bout time fer Tom and Cliff to git in from Fot Mead yet?" Earl Ray shifted his weight from one foot to the other and then shuffled his feet nervously.

"I reckon hit are bout time. They done been gone nye on to five day now. But we don't know whut they got their selves into tryin to drive the Texas bull through the scrub. We'uns jist gonna wait a spell more, I reckon," Jeremiah tried to soothe Earl Ray's jitters.

At about noon the next day, there was a noise in the scrub. At first, the hands thought it was a stampede, but no cattle lowing was heard. Then, with a terrible crashing sound, a huge bull burst though the palmettos with Cliff in tow. He had roped the beast and tried to lead it through the scrub. Out of desperation, he had cracked his whip. As a result, the huge bull panicked and charged headfirst through the scrub.

Since the rope was so tight, Cliff could not unwind it from his saddle horn. The bull was pulling the unwilling horse through the scrub, with Cliff hanging on in the saddle.

The hands quickly started cracking their whips, and the bull stopped in his tracks. One of the hands ran to the corral gate and threw it open. The bull was herded into the corral.

"Did y'all ever see horns that big? Them thangs muss be six or seven foot long. Hain't no wonder that critter makes so much noise in the scrub. We musta heared hit comin a mile back," John Henry spoke in an almost falsetto voice with the excitement of seeing the Texas bull coming through the Bent Penny clearing.

The bull was an impressive animal as it strode back and forth in the corral. Mr. Allbritton and the ladies paraded outside to get a closer look at the bull. Shaking his head, Mr. Allbritton exclaimed, "You boys know… that's a fine animal, and I hope it will do what you want it to breed some of the wild out of the scrub cattle. You're going to need to keep the scrub bulls away from him because they will try to gore each other. They're still wild animals at heart, you know."

With all the excitement, no one noticed that Tom was not with Cliff and the bull. When they had time to ask, Cliff was standing next to Blossom and the baby. Blossom was looking at Cliff with pleading eyes. And as Earl Ray, Jeremiah, and Mr. Allbritton came up, he was asked, "Cliff, where is Tom? Is he alright? What happened?"

Cliff looked down at Blossom as tears welled up in her eyes. Instinctively, she knew that Tom was in trouble. Then, he said. "Well, you see, we had got to Fote Mead and was attemptin to find that there cow seller man. When we found him, he was in McGorkles Saloon. We hain't had no food fer a day, so we thought we could git some vittles there since the stage stop was closed. Tom went in first, and I was right a hind em. We cain't see in thar, so's we'un jist stood by the door fer a few minutes til we'uns could see. Finally, Tom went to the bar and asked iffen that there feller was thar. He was. The barkeep pointed at em, so we went over to his table to talk. Jist as we done got to the table; two crackers started a noisy rumpus a hind us. Tom turned roun to see whut was happening when one of the cowboys drawed out his pistol and shot that other feller he was a fightin with. Somehow, that bullet got that cowboy and done shot poor Tom, too. He hain't dead. He jist hurt some bad. That thar bullet hit him in the side at his spare rib. It stayed in his shirt, and it was still hot. So it blistered his skin, too, I reckon. Anyhow, he bees at the saloon upstairs, in one of the whore's rooms. She done give er bed an livelihood up fer Ole Tom. They hain't no doc thar at that thar place, so I skint out fer Fote Blount and fetch me a doc to doctor Tom up some, don't you know."

Blossom was weeping openly, so Mary and Willie Mae were both consoling her. She kept saying in her Indian-English, "Me go! Me go! Me go, Tom. Baby go, Tom. He got have Blossom, and Baby. Me go."

"John Henry, go hitch the wagon and git the blankets from out of the chest," Willie Mae ordered her husband. John Henry turned on his heels and was soon driving the wagon out of the stable and into the yard.

"Come on, Blossom. Let's get you and the baby ready to go to Fort Mead." Mary took Blossom by the hand and led her to the house. Willie Mae followed, carrying little Bill in her arms.

Still in shock over Tom, Cliff kept telling Jeremiah, "I don't know whut I cudda did to hep Tom some more. I jist feel awful bout him. I jist gotta git back an see iffen he be all right."

Finally on their way, the wagon labored through the sand ruts. The mules seemed slower than usual, as the little band of travelers made their way toward Fort Blount. After that, they planned to turn south to Fort Mead.

The two days on the trail took its toll on them. Tired as they were, they still kept traveling toward Fort Mead, even through the night again. Since they left Bent Penny, they had stopped only once to fix some dinner for Blossom and Little Bill.

As fate would have it though, the doctor recognized Cliff and flagged him down, "Are you looking for your friend, Tom? Then come with me, and I'll take you to him. You see, I got him strong enough to move him and brought him here to my office where I could watch over him better. Oh, he's doing fine and will be able to travel in a day or so if he won't have to ride a horse."

"No sir, he hain't got no horse to ride, Doc. He gonna hafta ride in the wagon with his wife and youngun," John Henry said, and pulled the mules up so that Cliff could talk to the doctor.

The small troupe climbed the stairs into the doctor's office and found Tom in the doctor's bed. He was elated to see Blossom and Bill and glad to see Cliff and John Henry, too.

"How ya a feelin Tom? Do hit hurt very much?" Cliff asked as he walked to the foot of the bed to allow Blossom to kneel beside Tom and let him hold Bill for a while. The others mostly stood in silence as

Blossom spoke in Seminole, and Tom spoke in English. But they seemed to understand each other very well.

As Cliff and John Henry stepped into the doctor's office to let Tom and his family alone, the doctor motioned them over to his desk. There was a telegram which he read to Cliff and John Henry.

"All Texas cattle to be quarantined for a period of twenty one days. Stop. Tick fever rampant in Texas. Stop. Do not let any cattle come near other cattle or horses, mules, domestic donkeys. Stop. Look for red spots on humans and treat accordingly. Stop. All cases must be reported to Washington D.C. by a licensed physician. Stop. Signed United States of America Surgeon General, Washington D.C."

"What do hit mean, this here tellygram, Doctor?" asked Cliff as John Henry's mouth dropped open.

"It means that bull I heard that you drove from Fort Mead to your ranch may be infected with the Texas tick which causes tick fever in humans. It is almost always fatal to any animals which come in contact with the infected animal," the doctor answered with a sigh.

"It means that I will have to examine each of you before you leave my office. If all is okay, then you can go back to your ranch and prepare to dip your cattle and other animals to kill any ticks they have on them. Every three months, they will have to be dipped again," he continued.

"What do we dip'm in?" Cliff asked.

"I'll give you a formula and the proper chemicals to put into the water of your dipping vat. Here is a drawing of what a dipping vat should look like. If you build it like the plan says, it will be deep enough to dip your horses and mules. And remember, you must dip every cow that comes onto that ranch, also."

John Henry said, "Mummm… dat sho'gonna be a heap o' water toten a bucket at the time."

The doctor laughed, "You'll need to drive a well and put a pump there to pump into the vat. And even that will mean a lot of pumping to fill that pit."

Two days later, the doctor had examined each of the travelers and found them healthy. He admonished them to be sure and have every person on the ranch checked. If any signs show up, they should be treated immediately.

Four days on the trail again brought them to Bent Penny, and everyone present turned out to meet them to see how Tom was doing.

Cliff shouted to them. "Don't chall come too close to us. We gotta warnin from that there doctor. You need to know this cus it might kill you'ins." He handed the copy of the telegram to Mr. Allbritton to read. After reading it, Mr. Allbritton let his hands fall to his side and became flushed.

Jeremiah asked, "Whut is it? Whut's wrong?"

"Well Jeremiah and Earl Ray, your Texas bull is carrying Texas tick fever, and we have all been exposed to it. Now Mary and I will examine each of you. We will do this right now. All you men except Tom, Cliff, and John Henry, go to the bunk house. Cliff, you and John Henry see to Tom and Blossom. Take them to their cabin and, for the time being, stay there."

It had been eleven days since the bull had been brought to Bent Penny Cow Pens, and the gestation period for humans was fourteen days. At this time, no one had any symptom of the fever.

Mr. Allbritton supervised the digging of the pit. It was hard going, as boards had to be put into place to keep the dirt from caving in on the diggers. When the pit was just right, cypress boards were nailed to the sides and bottom to form a boat-like vessel. Next, hot pitch was poured onto the bottom boards and mopped onto the sides of the vat until it was waterproof and able to retain the many gallons of dip solution.

After that, a well was driven beside the vat. When the water was clear of sand, the pumping was started. Day and night the hands manned the pump and would spell each other after about thirty minutes.

Two days and one night later, the pit was full of water and chemicals were added. Copper, Paris green, creosote, coal oil, and lye soap were the chemicals that would kill the ticks on contact. If the ticks fell off on the ground, they would be sterile, so no harm would come from them.

The horses were driven through first. Since John Henry was the strongest man on the place, he was at the center and would use a large board with a round notch in it to push the animal's head down below the solution.

Jeremiah told Earl Ray and Mr. Allbritton, "I shore wish we had a digged that thar pit more away from the clearing. Hit don't smell purty no mo here. Hit stink lack that creosote and coal oil."

They all agreed and went on with the dipping.

The first day or two, no one had much of an appetite because of the odor of the dipping. Since they were wearing it on their clothes, too, they stayed in the odor all the time.

Finally, Willie Mae said, "Ya'll take them clothes off and throw em in the wash pot. I'm a gonna bile the stink outen them rags. And if that won't work, I'll bury em fer a few days, then wash em again. I jist cain't stand that smell no more."

The line of long underwear-clad men stretched out, and no other work was done until they had their work clothes back on.

They were fed in the bunkhouse, and though no one had any money, they spent the time playing poker until Willie Mae announced that they could line up and get their clothes from the clothes lines.

Now, came the time for all the men to bathe and wash out the underwear. That went over with mixed feeling even though they did have warm water in the barrel. First, the men would take off the long johns and hand them over the curtain to Willie Mae and John Henry. Next, the clothing was boiled, rinsed, soaped, and rinsed again before being hung on the clothes line to dry. Again, the men waited, clean and naked, in the bunkhouse.

In due time, the bull was let into the pasture with the scrub cow who were dipped and clean, ready to meet their new mate. Later that year, there was little disappointment in the services rendered by that Texas tick-free longhorn there at Bent Penny Cow Pens.

CHAPTER FOURTEEN

CRACKERS AND THE FIGHT

"Shut your tater mashin' hole, you ignorant..." The blaze of Jeremiah's ire only worsened when a fist stopped his sentence short.

"Now you shouldn'ta done that, you whisker-jawed catfish. Jist let me git up from here, and me and you gonna go at it tuther way round." Jeremiah scrambled to his feet after being knocked to the dirt by a cowboy he had just met.

He didn't know the cowboy's name, but he would not listen to a fellow ill-speak about any of his friends, and Tom was a special one.

The two men hunched over, facing each other, and started sidling in a circle. Jeremiah kept looking into his opponent's eyes. If he started to jab, Jeremiah would duck and plant an upper cut on the cowboy's chin. He feigned a left. Then, when the cowboy took the bait, he came from knee height with the upper cut. The punch landed hard, and Jeremiah felt the power of the blow all the way to his shoulder.

"Gunnuh," croaked the cowboy, and the back of his head hit the ground first. He just lay there not moving for several minutes. Then Jeremiah picked up his hat from the sand rut, went to the horse trough, dipped a hat full of water, and then poured it in the cowboys face. He sputtered and spit, then coughed. As he started to get up, Jeremiah held out his hand; and the cowboy took the assistance with a bit of malice.

The cowboy took another swing at Jeremiah, but Jeremiah backed out of the way. And while he still had the man's hand, twirled him like a whip. Next, Jeremiah's boot heel caught the side of the cowboy's left knee. A loud snap was heard, and the cowboy was once more on the ground, holding his leg and moaning.

"Now you kin jist lie there. I ain't a gonna give you no mo chances to hit me no mo," Jeremiah told the man. He then turned to Tom and Cliff with orders, "Drag him outen of the middle of the dirt street so he don't git runned over." Aggravated, Jeremiah stepped over to the sidewalk and started down to the general store.

The Kissimmee town marshal was notified that there was a fight in the middle of Main Street, so he walked down the street to see what was going on for himself. The marshal asked the cowboy what had happened, and he answered with a loud, painful groan.

"Did you see what happened to this old boy here in the dirt?" the marshal asked Tom and Cliff, as they had just finished dragging the man to the edge of the street.

"I reckon that Jeremiah took most of the fight outen of 'im, but he started it all by a callin Tom here a liar. And Tom hain't ever said a lie in his life. I know, cuz I done growed up with Tom here," Cliff told the marshal. Then he added, "Jeremiah tole this feller to hush up his tator hole, and the man slugged Jeremiah. Jeremiah don't cotton to bein hit lack that an specially from no stranger. So Jeremiah don cold cocked tha feller then he tried to help him offen the dirt, and this here booger done swang at him agin. That's when Jeremiah horse-kicked that feller in the knee, and I thank hit's busted, fer we heard a sharp snap, and he went back in the dirt. Then Jeremiah axed me and Tom to drag him out of the road lessen he git runned over by somebody."

"Okay," said the marshal. Then he turned to Tom and said, "You go fetch the doctor and let him see what this feller needs. Then I'll put him in jail."

The town marshal was Ellwood McElroy. He spent twenty years with the Pinkerton Detective Agency and had retired with a pension which consequently he soon found would not keep him alive very long.

Traveling from Chicago, Illinois to Florida, when he heard there was need for law enforcement in Kissimmee, so he rode into town and applied for the job.

His first time in the small cow town was mostly quiet. Seldom did he have to leave his office, the café, or the saloon because of any crime. It was mostly fights between drunken cowboys or an occasional dispute over a bull or a calf that wandered onto some other rancher's property.

He worked with the circuit judge, Knollwood Harrington, who came to the area every four months and held court where he also brought the town council up on the latest laws concerning townships, what taxes were new or had to be repealed, plus all other legal matters. Then the judge would travel to another town and so forth, until he was back in Kissimmee again.

It was about a week before the judge was due in town, so marshal McElroy would hold any prisoners over until he arrived.

Judge Harrington, had sworn the marshal in as justice of the peace for the town and any surrounding towns that would like to have the pseudo judge hear less serious cases. So the marshal, sitting as the justice of peace, held court to hear the complaints which made it less demanding on the circuit judge's caseload.

After the doctor had placed a cast on the leg of the cowboy, the marshal had put him in the jailhouse and was going to hold the J.P. court the next day.

The marshal found Jeremiah at the general store and asked if he could stay over until about noon the next day. Jeremiah agreed. Then he, Tom, and Cliff went over to the hotel for a room that night.

Before they settled in to rest, they went to the café and ate supper, then sat outside the general store until it closed at sundown. Finding the mosquitoes, deer flies, and yellow flies too much of a nuisance, they went into the hotel where screen doors kept the pests at bay. If they had been in the scrub, they would have dabbed on some coal oil or naptha, which repelled the pests, then turned into their bedroll and gone to sleep. But they were in town and didn't want the lingering odor of the insect repellent on their town clothes.

The next morning found the trio up and waiting for the café to open. The smell of coffee permeated the hotel lobby and really whetted their appetite for breakfast. Soon the manager opened the hotel lobby to the café. Three hungry cowboys quickly entered, and ordered coffee and breakfast.

Just as the coffee arrived at their table, they heard a familiar voice. Turning around they spotted Mr. Allbritton walking toward their table.

Greeting him, Jeremiah said, "Drag up a chair. You're jist in time fer a cup of coffee and breakfast. When did you git back in town? How was your trip? We ain't got much time to talk but we sure are glad you're back now." Then he added, "You know I'm a gonna go into court today. Yep, the justice of the peace has spoke and said that there feller I done whuped yestiday got his leg broke in the scuffle. Now that fool wants me to pay him good money cuz he cain't cowboy fer a spell. Now can you believe that?"

Mr. Allbritton said, "Yes, Jeremiah. I heard about your altercation last night when I got off the stagecoach. I spent the night in the hotel, too, and thought you all might like to have some company while you are here. And… I'll stand up for you if you need me to."

"Well, thanks, Mr. Allbritton. I was kinda wonderin whut wuz a gonna happen to me, and ah really hain't never been inside no courtroom afore. Ah hain't skeered none ah jist wish I knowed whut the J.P.'s gonna do bout me fighten at ere feller. You know Mr. Allbritton, I hain't never laid narry a eyeball on that feller afore."

"Well now, Jeremiah, don't worry too much about the guy suing you because the marshal said that the cowboy struck the first blow. That means that he is at fault and the J. P. will most likely throw that out of court, giving the cowboy jail time for disturbing the peace."

Tom and Cliff had not said anything after the greeting of Mr. Allbritton. They had just listened to what Jeremiah and Mr. Allbritton were talking about.

Mr. Allbritton turned to Tom and asked, "What did the man say that set Jeremiah off so?"

"Well sir, I know you knowed that me and that Injun woman we found in the scrub having a baby, that her and me got hitched. Now some o them call me a squaw man. Well, I can live with at, but that feller said I done stole his woman and that the baby was his. Then, he said we done stole her from her people. We ain't done no such a thang, Mr. Allbritton. We done found'er in the scrub a havin a baby lack I done said. Then the feller called me a liar. Before I could turn around, Jeremiah, here, done started a yellin at him to shut his tater trap. That's when he done cold-cocked Jeremiah. After Jeremiah got up off the ground, he hit the feller with a uppercut and knocked him clean cold. After that, Jeremiah got a hat full o water out of the horse trough and throwed it in the feller's face. Well, he come to, and Jeremiah tried to help him off the ground when the fool tried to hit Jeremiah agin, and Jeremiah tried to help him an that's when Jeremiah don hoss kicked em in the leg. The doctor says hit's broke."

"You know, Jeremiah, from what Tom told me, and Cliff agreed with him by nodding all through his explanation, I don't think the J.P. is going to even keep you in court today. Anyhow, I'll have a talk with marshal McElroy before puts on his J.P. hat."

"Well Mr. Allbritton, I'm mighty happy to hear that you'll stand up fer me in the court. And I reckon I'll jist bout do anything to git this here done with," Jeremiah said and then poured coffee all around.

At sun up the marshal unlocked the cell door and took the cowboy prisoner some breakfast. As he entered the cell, he noticed that the man wasn't breathing and was very pale. He put the tray down and tried to rouse him.

It was too late. He was dead.

Then he saw the large pool of blood under the cot and found that he had slashed his wrists during the night.

"I'm telling you, now, you done save the town a heap o money by croaking yourself like that," the marshal said. Then he picked up the tray, locked the cell door, and murmured to himself, "Ain't no use locking that door because he ain't going no where."

Then he sat down at his desk in the office and ate the prisoner's breakfast.

CHAPTER FIFTEEN

CRACKERS IN THE SWAMP

"Don't make no noise an hit'll come up. Then we'uns kin throw a rope on em," Jeremiah told Tom.

"I ain't got no intention to move lessen hit's a headed this a way. Then I'm a goin the tuther direction," Tom exclaimed.

"Jeremiah, how big you reckon that thar gator is got to be?" Tom asked. Then added, "I reckon hit mus be a nigh to foteen foot, or so, don't cha thank?"

Jeremiah stood frozen as the huge alligator eased through the murky water of the swamp. There seemed to be no end to the length, as it swam by cypress knees and grass. Jeremiah thought of the old rule of thumb that the bulk of the gator, as it was thought, the distance between his eyes in inches would be equal to its length in feet. This was a very big gator.

"I reckon hits bout foteen foot, maybe less. But iffen I kin git this here lasso on im, hit won't eat no more cow critters," Jeremiah whispered back to Tom.

It hadn't been that long since the panther attack, and Jeremiah was still a little stiff from the torn muscles in his shoulder. He really didn't want to capture the beast but would rather shoot it between the eyes and let it stay in the swamp. However, Tom was determined to eat the meat and sell the hide. That would also give some payback because the gator had killed at least three calves and one cow.

The gator was still silently swimming toward the cow heart that they had suspended above the water just out of reach of the gator's jaws. Suddenly, the alligator stopped, then eyed the beef heart, moved back a few inches, and lunged for the prize just beyond its grasp.

The lasso made a perfect circle around the alligator's neck when it splashed back in the water and disappeared in the cloud of mud the commotion had created. Two wraps with the rope around the cypress sapling and the fight was on, as the alligator discovered that it was caught.

With a roll and a thunderous whip of his giant tail, the alligator fought. The rope was taut around its neck and was now restricting its breathing. More rolls and more splashing occurred until it lay quiet in the muddy water.

Tom reached to take the rope. As he did, the alligator started to roll and then ran headlong onto the bank where Jeremiah and Tom were standing. Frightened, Jeremiah turned and fled toward the clearing, as Tom started backing away from the gator. Then the unthinkable happened. Tom tripped over a cypress knee in the water and fell backward into the tannic liquid. The alligator then ran directly over Tom. As it reached the end of its tether, it jerked back over Tom's frame. Still tied, the alligator continued in the direction of the swamp and was unaware that it had been so near one of its antagonists.

Jeremiah ran back to the place where Tom had gone under and felt around for what he was sure would be Tom's lifeless body. As the gator reached the end of its rope, it again turned and lay still in the swamp water.

Just then, Tom emerged blowing like a porpoise and caught his breath. He had swum nearly twenty feet from where he had fallen.

Rushing to his side, Jeremiah asked if he was hurt and found no harm had come to Tom. He then grabbed his belt and drug him toward the edge of the water.

"I'm a gonna git the Winchester and shoot at that dang gator. We'uns hain't a gonna git that booger out no tuther way, no how," Jeremiah said as he was running toward his horse which was tied a safe distance away.

He returned with the gun and waited for the alligator to surface again so he could be sure where the shot would hit him. However, the alligator did not resurface. He tugged on the rope, and there was no longer any fight in that reptile. He and Tom pulled again on the rope which had enough to wrap the rope around another tree.

Tom said, "Why don't we'uns tie your rope to this un, an I thank my horse kin pull the gator critter out of the swamp."

Jeremiah was still leery of the alligator and was about to refuse when Tom came up with a rope, leading his own horse. He quickly tied the ends of the rope together and kept one loop around the small cypress tree.

Tom spurred the horse on and soon the gator was up to the loop at the tree. The ropes were untied and they felt it was safe enough to drag the alligator into the clearing. As it approached land, the horse could no longer pull the huge alligator. They then incorporated Jeremiah's horse, and soon the alligator was on dry land.

Jeremiah put a forty-five bullet in the alligator's head to make sure it was dead. Then he asked, "How we'uns gonna butcher this here gator, Tom?"

Tom was pacing the length of the alligator and whistled, then said, "Jeremiah, this here critter done be fifteen foot and some more. I reckon we'uns cain't hang em from no oak er hicker tree cuz we'uns hain't that tall. No we'uns hain't," Then eying the full length said, "We'uns kin turn em on his back an skin em , I reckon."

Jeremiah suggested, "Let's go to the house an git John Henry an the wagon. We'uns kin skin an butcher em thar."

"All right, I'll stay here iffen y'all don't care and keep the buzzards from a pickin at em." Tom told Jeremiah.

Jeremiah was gone about two hours before he returned with John Henry driving the wagon. John Henry drove over near the gator and stared a long time at the animal.

"Ooo, wee! Y'all sho cotched the granddaddy of all tha gators in the world," John Henry shouted, "I cain't wait to git some o him in my teeth. I knows Willie Mae gonna cook us a mess o gator dis evenin. How much y'all thank hit'll weigh? I would reckon bout two bale o cotton er mo," he continued, "We uns gonna hafta cut em in half cut em in haf to git em in da wagon. Whut choo thank, Mista Tom?"

"Well, John Henry, I hain't want to cut em I want to sell the hide in one piece. Feller in Fort Blount'll pay two dolla a foot fer a critter hide this here big," Tom declared as he eyed the catch.

"Mista Tom, we uns kin skin em here and cut the meat half in two. I knows we'uns cain't put that big thang in the wagon whole, though." Then he asked, "Ya'll don't wont the guts. That'll weigh bout a hunert pound. Then the buzzards kin eat, too," John Henry figured with Jeremiah as which was the best way to get the bulk of the gator meat and the uncut hide back to Bent Penny Cow Pens.

"Let's do er then, and git out of his here swamp. The skeeters an yeller flies is about to tote me an my hoss off," Jeremiah agreed.

Tom was still somewhat wet when he arrived at his cabin door. John Henry pulled the wagon under the butchering shed while Jeremiah put his horse in the stable and started rubbing him down. A chill went over him, and he shuddered, "What would I have done if things had gone bad with that gator runnin head long over Tom?" He mused as he went to the wash stand and washed his hands and face. That way, he camouflaged his tears of fright and thankfulness.

Willie Mae brought a large dish pan with her to the shed where the gator meat was being cut up and prepared for cooking. She took the pan, brimming full of meat, and went back into the kitchen.

Blossom and Billy met Tom at the door of the, cabin. When she saw the mess Tom was in, she looked at him as if to say, "How did you get so wet and dirty." She took his clothes out to the wash pot and started washing them while he dressed. Tom played with Billy on the cabin floor which caused Blossom to be very contented. She loved to see her two boys playing like young deer in the scrub.

An hour later, the bell rang out as the first call to dinner. Willie Mae served everyone while more alligator fried in the large skillet. Along with the alligator, she had prepared okra and tomatoes, rice, grits, biscuits, and coffee. Also, Mary had baked her delicious pecan pie.

All were laughing at the yarn Tom was spinning about the capture of the alligator that was going down into stomachs well, and the way Tom swam under water to escape the alligator, only to have him run over him, not once, but twice. Tom related how the alligator's trouncing him only gave his swimming strokes more power.

Jeremiah and Blossom smiled but were not as elated as the others, for it was far from a joke to them. However, they were very happy the story ended happily for Tom.

The day had ended well as the sun slipped down into the scrub at Bent Penny Cow Pens.

CHAPTER SIXTEEN

CRACKER ENGINEER TAKES A WIFE

David Crockett Pierce had built himself a small cabin near the salt pond and had gone to Savannah to bring back his engineering equipment which he had stored and was needing back at the Bent Penny Cow Pens.

His wagon was filled to the top hardly leaving room for anything else. In addition, there was this and there was that which he would surely need in Florida. It was best to take it now because the trip by railway freight might not get it to him unscathed.

"I've got enough stuff for two wagons, so I guess I'll have to buy another one," he thought as he surveyed the overloaded wagon. "Yeah, but if I do that, who am I going to get to drive a wagon all the way down to Florida?" he thought to himself as he scratched his head where it didn't itch and stuck his hand in his pocket.

"Oh my gosh! I totally forgot the note Mr. Allbritton gave me with the address of his friend. I wonder if I can slip the visit in and still finish my moving before it gets too cold up here," Davy wondered as he kept packing boxes and crates much the same as when he had moved from Brunswick, Georgia, a year and a half ago.

Davy was now turning twenty-five and was thrilled with the success of his surveying business. As a graduate engineer from M.I.T., he had previously been plying his profession in Savannah. Then, he had moved to central Florida and found a home there. At the present, he was feeling very anxious to return to his cabin by the salt pond.

Feeling pangs of guilt obligated him to go visit Mr. Allbritton's old friend, Mr. Wendell Hampton, as he had promised.

Davy closed his shop door and went upstairs to the apartment over the shop which he had been sharing with his old friend, Bob Tacket. As he washed up and dressed, Bob came in and asked Davy, "Where are you going all dressed to the nines?"

Davy told him that he had promised Mr. Allbritton that he would visit his old army friend, and it had slipped his mind until he found the note in his pocket this afternoon.

"I really need to be packing and getting ready for the trip to Florida, Bob; however, I guess I can make this effort since I know that Mr. Allbritton would do it for me," Davy murmured.

Davy stepped onto the sidewalk and hailed a cabriolet. As he climbed in he gave the driver the address and admired the elegantly hooded, one-horse carriage.

They had traveled into the squares. On one corner, they noticed a young lady trying to hail a cab. Davy asked the driver to pull over to the curb, and he offered the services of his cab to the young lady. She gladly accepted and climbed in the hack with an arm load of bundles. Placing them on the seat facing Davy, she stuck out her hand to shake Davy's hand.

"I'm Brittany Hampton. Whom do I have the pleasure of sharing this ride?" Stunned by her incredible beauty, Davy simply shook her hand. Finally trying to get his words together, he stammered, "I…I'm… my name is David Crocket Pierce, and I am so happy to meet you, Mrs. Hampton."

Brittany laughed, "No I am *MISS* Hampton. I'm not married and I am happy to meet you, Mr. David Crocket Pierce." Davy settled in for the ride and remembered the piece of paper he had in his pocket. After reading it again, he asked, "Are you perhaps of the Wendell Hampton family?"

Brittany looked at him in a strange way, then said, "Why yes, he's my father. And how do you come to know him?"

Davy related as to how Mr. Hampton and Mr. John Allbritton were friends and that he had met him at Bent Penny Cow Pens.

As the ride went on, the better acquainted the two became. The hack pulled the cab up to the curb and the driver announced, "You are here sir."

Davy stared in awe at the mansion and asked Brittany, "You mean that people actually live in this huge place?"

"Yes, Mr. David Crocket Pierce. This is my home, sweet home and has been for the last nineteen years. Come on now and let me introduce you to my family," she said warmly. Davy watched admiringly as she practically floated from the cab. He paid the cabby and gathered up the bundles which Brittany had deposited on the seat, then followed her to the door.

As the door opened, he saw the cavernous entry and thought, "I could get used to living like this, but perhaps not on an engineer's pay."

After the introductions, Davy was escorted into the game room which had so impressed Mr. Allbritton.

Mr. and Mrs. Hampton were great hosts. Soon Davy was feeling at home with his new found friends. They invited him to have dinner with them and he accepted although he felt he was not dressed for such a formal home and what he thought would be a grand formal dinner.

The meal was complete with cigars and brandy in the game room. As the evening wore on, he wondered what Brittany was doing and if he would get to see her again before he left Savannah.

That was a moot question. As soon as it had entered his mind, Brittany came bounding through the door. Taking Davy by the hand, she said, "Come along, Mr. David Crocket Pierce. We have to get out of this place and go where the lights are bright." Mr. Hampton nodded his agreement and went to the side of the room to pull a rope. In a moment, a butler came into the room. Mr. Hampton ordered his buggy be hitched and readied for the young couple to use for the evening.

The buggy was comfortable and the horses were sleek. It was a rig to be proud of and to be seen in.

Soon they were in front of a grand hotel. From inside came the strains of an orchestra. As they went in, the man at the desk recognized Davy and spoke to him as he went by. Davy spoke and in the greeting asked him about the dance.

"It's not a fancy ball, and you are dressed just fine. If you and the lady want to dance, go right in and find a table. I'll tell you what. Let me go and get you all a good table near the orchestra." He was gone only a couple of minutes and returned with the head waiter who escorted them to a vacant table near the bandstand.

Davy ordered lemonade because he was sure they would not serve champagne to Brittany since she was still underage, he thought. The waiter came to the table with champagne and an ice bucket to chill it in. He placed a stemmed glass in front of each of them and poured the wine. Davy was awe struck! He had never had such great service in his life.

He thought now, "I know for certain that I could get used to this life."

Soon it was nearly midnight; Davy was getting tired because he had been packing the wagon since early morning. The band played their final waltz as Davy and Brittany clung to each other and hated for the evening to end.

Now, riding in the buggy, they passed a square in town where there was a fountain in a small park. Brittany asked for Davy to pull over so that they could stroll through the park for a few minutes.

Watching the fountain water dance, Davy felt Brittany slip her hand into his. He clasped her small, warm hand and felt that if he let her go he would drop totally dead right there on the spot.

Brittany turned to face Davy and said, "Mr. David Crocket Pierce, have you had an enjoyable evening?"

Davy said, "Please will you just call me Davy. I really like that better.... And I will call you Brittany, if I may."

"I would be too delighted, Davy, and would you mind if I stood closer to you? I'm a little chilled."

Davy slipped his arm around her tiny waist and pulled her close. As he did, she faced him and asked, "Davy, will you kiss me?"

Davy was dumbfounded and before he could say yes, no, maybe, they were locked in their first embrace.

"Let's go home now, Davy. I need to think about what I have just boldly done and need to ponder what you might think of me in the morning," Brittany exclaimed,

Later, there was a knock on the door at Davy's apartment, and he looked around for his roommate. Bob was gone already. Next, Davy looked at the clock beside the bed. It was almost nine o'clock. He quickly slipped on his robe and went barefoot to the door to find one of the butlers from the Hampton's house. He handed Davy a note and then turned around. As an afterthought, he turned back and asked, "Will there be an answer Sir?" Davy quickly read the note and said, "No, Sir. I'll attend to this immediately."

Davy dressed and quickly went to the street to hail a cab. He told the cabby the address of the Hampton's and was still in deep thought when the cab pulled up in front of the mansion. Davy thought he was in deep trouble for letting Brittany drink the champagne or for keeping her out too late. All these questions and thoughts kept racing through his mind. Now, here he was at their home and ready to face whatever was coming to him.

Brittany answered the door and was bubbling over. She grabbed Davy and gave him a hug, then with him in hand took him to the patio where her father and mother were about to have breakfast.

"Davy, won't you have breakfast with us? We hope you haven't eaten so you will have a good appetite," Mrs. Hampton stated.

"Why, yes Ma'am, I am rather hungry and appreciate you asking me," Davy answered, although he was still uneasy as to why he had been summoned to the Hampton mansion, other than to have breakfast.

Mr. Hampton talked to Davy about being an engineer, what he had done, and where he had been since he graduated from the University of Georgia.

Davy told them about being hired as a surveyor for the railroad and how he had met Mr. Allbritton, Jeremiah, and Earl Ray. He told them of his experience at the salt plant and how it was paying off. Without wanting to boast, he described the cabin he had and that he was moving to central Florida to be a civil engineer.

Mr. Hampton asked if he and Davy could have a private conversation. Davy agreed soon they were alone in the game room.

"Davy, we asked you here this morning to see if you had feelings for Brittany. When she came home last night she informed us that she was going to marry you," Mr. Hampton said in a very fatherly way.

Davy was awe struck and completely taken by the surprise. "I have very deep feelings for Brittany, and I would surely like to have her for my wife. I am just starting out on my own and I haven't much to offer her as a hearth and home sir."

"Well, just don't be too hasty to shortchange yourself. You come highly recommended by John Allbritton, and really that is enough for me," Mr. Hampton proclaimed, then added, "I know that you have known Brittany for only a few hours, but she is heart set on getting married to you, and soon."

"Yes sir, I practically worship the ground that Mr. Allbritton walks on. Yet I..."

Davy's words trailed off as Wendell Hampton was gazing at him with his stern eyes and then said, "David, you graduated from the Massachusetts Institute of Technology. You earned your degree by working hard and keeping your hand in your surveying while in school. You are a hard worker, and you know where you are going. Your goals are set, and it seems that you do not wish to be turned from that path. That is commendable and you should be given a lot of credit for your aims. And yet, you are missing something from you life… you're missing life, David, and you shouldn't. You have so much to offer the world, yet you don't see it," he paused and looked straight into Davy's eyes.

"Look around you, my boy, and see for yourself what can be done when you apply all that enthusiasm and hard work toward your goals. This house, my foundry, and all the things a person could want. And I am ashamed of myself, David. Yes, I am ashamed of myself. For once I stood about where you are standing. I, too, was in love with the daughter of the richest man in Savannah. I gave into the human side of me and became what I am today, on the back of my wife's and my father-in-law's fortune," he continued, looking away.

"Oh, I could have made it on my own, but this was the way I chose. This is where I will stay. But you, lad, you can be so much more than I am or ever will be if you will just stick to that dream of yours,"

Wendell looked now as though he were Davy's father and finished by saying, "I have not and will not offer you my foundry business nor my daughter's hand, less I corrupt you and your dream. Take Brittany as your wife and take her to your paradise in Florida. There you will most likely build your own empire. You certainly have the ability and guts to go after whatever it is that you want."

"Brittany, will you come into the game room please," Wendell called.

Brittany entered the room and looked at Davy. She lowered her head, walked up to him, took his hand, and they both looked at Wendell, who was studying their faces as he glanced from Davy to his daughter. Then with tearing eyes, he said, "David Crocket Pierce, I give you and Brittany my richest and hardiest blessings. I hope you will give each other the happiness and the family you both deserve. God bless you both. Now get out of here and go make plans for your wedding. And remember always that your mother and I love you deeply. And you, too, Davy."

The steamboat huffed and puffed up to the pier. The gang plank was lowered and the crowd started down the plank to the dock.

This was the second visit made by Mr. John Allbritton in two years. However, now, he was going to see his best friend give his only child and daughter to his other best friend, Davy. As he approached the door to the terminal, he spied Davy and Brittany waiting at the gate. Hurrying to them, he shook Davy's hand, then took Brittany into his strong arms and gave her a big bear hug. They made their way to the outside and to the carriage waiting out front. They climbed in, and Mr. Allbritton said, "Shouldn't I see about my baggage?"

Davy said, "No Sir. Old Will Henry will pick it up and bring it to the house for you. All you have to do is sit back and enjoy the Savannah fall day,"

"Old Will Henry? Is he still living in these parts?" Mr. Allbritton asked.

"Yessir, and he will be driving one of our wagons to Florida, when we leave next week," Davy said, as he watched Mr. Allbritton's face to see if he could detect a modicum of approval.

Mr. Allbritton turned his eyes to Brittany and asked, "Just what do you think you are going to do with my almost son, Brittany? And I have actually begun to see him as the son I never had but wanted so badly."

Brittany looked lovingly at Davy and said, "I'll think of something, Mr. Allbritton. I'll think of something," and they laughed as the coach drew up to the mansion.

Almost a month later, the little caravan drew up into the yard of the Bent Penny Cow Pens to the cheers and applause of all the hands. Jeremiah, Earl Ray, and Mary welcomed the pair as Blossom gave Brittany a necklace of beads she had made from seeds growing around the scrub.

Blossom said, "Kopti make you make lots of baby," and she went back to Tom's side.

Everyone laughed and indicated that it was working for them since Blossom was noticeably pregnant with her second child.

It seemed as though everyone had come to the Bent Penny compound to see the new bride and groom. There were covered wagons, tents, tepees, and other forms of shelter set up. There must have been a hundred people who came to the party that Mr. Allbritton and Mary had put together for Davy and Brittany.

When Brittany entered the main house for the first time, there stood her mother and father. The surprise was complete. She ran to them and wrapped her arms around her parents. They all laughed and cried and hugged and hugged some more.

The dinning hall was decorated with magnolias and other wild flowers that made the room smell like a garden. In the center of the hall, the long table was beginning to sway with the load of food that it was burdened with. Even a whole steer was being roasted over an oak and hickory fire in the yard.

Between the bunk house and the tack shed, a brand new floor had been built. It would first be used as a dance floor. When someone asked what it would be used for when the party was over, Mary answered, "I am going to build a schoolhouse to teach those hooligans how to read, write, and act like they had some kind of upbringing."

The party lasted all night. As the day broke, Davy pushed the door of his little cabin open with his toe with Brittany cradled in his arms and proceeded across the threshold. Then, he kicked the door closed with his boot heel and let her ease slowly to the floor. As the sun shone glimmering across the salt pond, Davy and Brittany embraced and kissed for the first time in their new Florida home.

Thereafter for a little while, all was still at Bent Penny Cow Pens.

CHAPTER SEVENTEEN

CRACKER TWINS

The spring of 1897 brought a lot of changes to Bent Penny Cow Pens. There were now several hundred cross-bred scrub cows with calves. The new breed had longer horns than normal scrub cows but were considerably shorter than those on the Texas bull. The steers were heavier and yielded more beef per head than the smaller and tougher scrub cow. Thus, a new breed of cattle was born at Bent Penny.

And now there were two children in the Tom and Blossom Walker's home, a boy and a girl. Billy was seven, and little Mary was three. Blossom named the little girl after Mary Sykes-Remmick, who Blossom always looked up to and tried to copy in all things. Blossom had become a great cook just like Mary and a fast learning student in the school. Her English was now better than most of the men, that included her husband.

Blossom and Tom were learning to read and write now at Mary Remmick's Bent Penny School. Jeremiah and Earl Ray were her first graduates. Now both could read and write more than just their names. Cliff Teague was in and out; as he would find any excuse to keep from going into that school. All-in-all the school was going well, and there were more and more ranch-hands children who were old enough to attend. From the surrounding scrub and small settlements, eight or ten more attended.

Mary's load was getting heavier with each passing month. It seemed that more people were settling around Lake Wailes now. Some of the children were being brought in by the wagon load and even the parents were staying while their child was educated. They, too, began to learn the value of an education.

Davy and Brittany Crocket had twin boys who were now almost one year old. The older boy (by a whole fifteen minutes) was named after his father, David. The second was named Johnny after John Allbritton. The twins became the very apple of Mr. Allbritton's eye. Every week or so he would remind Mary and Willie Mae that the twin's birthday was coming and that he wanted it to be a great party for the boys. His doting over them had become somewhat of a chore for Brittany because she tried to keep some sort of routine for them. However, Mr. Allbritton would come in and want to take them riding in the buggy or just bounce them on his knee. He was the greatest of grandfathers and would go to any length to see that the entire family was okay and didn't need anything.

Brittany had a lady, Maude Elsie Tanner, to help her. Maude and her husband, Spurgeon, ran a small store, stage coach line, and depot at one of the settlements. She would come in every day to help tend to the children. After every evening bath and supper was cooked, she would trudge off until the next day. Mr. Allbritton thought this was a waste of money until he had them to himself one day.

That plan was to let Mr. Allbritton see what a job it really was to keep up with the two boys who would sleep in shifts. When both were awake and in need of a bath or to be fed, each would run in the opposite direction, which doubled the time it took to round them up. Davy often recommended a lasso or small corral. "They are a handful," he would say.

Once they went to the cow pens and had taken off their clothes to play in the mud next to the watering trough. When Mary spied them from the schoolhouse window, she ran out and took them by the hands and turned them over to Mr. Allbritton to bathe and dress.

Mr. Allbritton soon realized that he was too old and the twins were too young for him to handle by himself. That brought an end to his chiding Brittany about Maude Elsie helping her.

For days at a time, Davy was gone to do engineering on the land surveys in and around Lake Wailes. There were several new towns that were plated, and the lay out was more difficult to complete because of the numerous natural lakes in this part of Florida. But he couldn't be happier. When he finally did arrive at home, he was the king of the house. The twins giggled and squealed as they played with their father.

While Davy and his crew surveyed an area, they would name the lakes after the men on the survey crew. Some of the lakes were named after presidents or famous people in the area; but, most were named after the crew.

When there was time, Blossom and Brittany would take the four children in hand and go for walks around the Bent Penny compound. To teach the children, they would point out different birds, plants and other animals. As they strolled, Blossom would explain in English and Seminole what each meant to her tribe and if they were good medicine or not. She would find a herb that the children could chew on and enjoy during the outing. One time she found a sassafras plant and let them chew on the bark. From then on, each time they went by that plant, they all wanted the "sweet wood." Often, they would take many of the leaves home and make tea for the ladies to sip and enjoy. Brittany was especially fond of the sassafras tea as it reminded her of her home in Savannah.

One day, little Billy found a small green snake and was holding it up to show little Mary. When Mary saw it at about the same time as Brittany, the snake was quickly taken in hand by Blossom who said, "It is important for the little child to know that there are good and bad in the land, some animals, some birds and some snakes. Now we must teach the children the bad ones, and the good ones will keep them safe, too."

Not knowing exactly what Blossom was saying, Brittany told the children, "Isn't it better to point out the snake than to pick it up and possibly be bitten? So for now on just show a grown-up what it is you want them to see and let the adult protect the child?"

One very lovely day, as they were walking thought the scrub, they took a path which they had never walked before. As they were walking and dodging palmetto leaves, little Billy noticed a cow that he said was tall. As they approached, they found that the cow was standing on top of an ancient Seminole burial mound. The mound was about twenty feet high. When Billy started to scamper up, Blossom said something in Seminole that caused him to stop in his tracks.

"What is this?" Brittany asked.

"It is the burial place of my ancestors," answered Blossom, as she knelt by the place and chanted a prayer to *Wakan Tanka,* her god, and then quietly stood and backed away from the spot.

The next day, she had Tom and Cliff build a fence around the burial mound. They seldom walked that way again so as not to disturb the souls of the ancestors who were entombed there. The fence also kept the cattle away from the mound and the scrub grew around the spot making it all but forgotten for years to come.

Brittany thought about the mound and how fitting it was to have discovered the shrine with the children and the education they received from hearing Blossom explain what was inside the mound. People are born to parents on the earth. Then when death comes to them, the children become parents, and the cycle continues. But the cycle of that Bent Penny burial mound remained frozen in the century in which it was closed to the eye of man forever.

The barbed wire fence was replaced with wrought fence and a gate to be left alone as a fitting protection for the shrine. Blossom was proud of the wrought iron fence and viewed it as a reward to her ancestors and their way of life in the Florida scrub.

Chapter Eighteen

MR. ALLBRITTON'S GRANDSON

The tall, well dressed stranger walked into the Sheriff's office in Fort Blount and asked the deputy, "Do you know a man by the name of John Allbritton?" The deputy leaned over to one side of the desk and spit out some of the tobacco juice, partially hitting the spittoon. Some hit the sawdust on the floor, which had been spread there for just such a miss as this.

"Who wants to know?" The deputy asked.

"I am John Brack, and I think that Allbritton is my grandfather." The young man said.

The deputy took another long look at the lad. In sizing him up, he thought aloud, "Yeah I can see the family resemblance, all right."

The young man had ridden up on a white stallion, with a black tooled saddle and bridle with a martingale to match. The saddle blanket was rich wool and had red and white piping around the outside. This was the horse and outfit of some rich dude from God knows where. And here he was in central Florida looking for Mr. Allbritton.

He stood six foot four and weighed about one hundred and eighty pounds. He was dressed in black from his hat to his boots with a white kerchief tied with a square knot around his neck and inside his open collar. He wore silver spurs on his boots with rowels that matched the star conchos on his saddle.

His two silver Colts were in a tooled, wide leather rig that showed the bone handles like the sun reflecting off of a lake. The bullet loops held an additional twenty four .45 caliber long Colt bullets, and both holsters were tied down in the manner of a quick-draw gun fighter.

His wide brim Stetson hat curled near the front, and the crown stood up with the crease in the center, domed in the back. He was a striking figure of a man and hardly the scrub cowboy type.

The deputy explained how to get to the Bent Penny Cow Pens and told him it was a two-day, hard ride from Fort Blount or a three-day easy ride.

The young man thanked the deputy and went over to the hotel café. The hotel was not as hot inside as the sheriff's office had been. The man walked to a table and sat down with his back to the wall.

He ordered dinner and coffee. When he had finished, he asked the waiter how much he owed.

The waiter said, "Four bits," and picked up the money as John Brack placed it on the table.

The three days it took for John to find the Bent Penny Cow Pens were uneventful. When he rode into the compound and straight up to the front door of the main house, he went to the office and found no one. He stepped next door and spoke out, "Anybody home?"

Willie Mae was in the kitchen and heard the voice as she went to the entry. Letting out a squeal of surprise at the stranger standing in the hall, she ran back into the kitchen and came back with Mary and Blossom.

The young man introduced himself and asked, "Is this where John Allbritton lives?"

Mary answered, "Yes, but during the day, he stays over at the Pierce place a mile down the lane past the cow pens and dipping vat. Do you want someone to fetch him for you?"

"No Ma'am. If you don't mind, I'll sit on the porch and wait for him to come up. I have business with him."

Along about dusk, Mr. Allbritton rode up in his buggy and got down as John Henry turned the horse around and headed for the stable.

Mr. Allbritton had taken the three steps up to the porch before he saw the young man. As he neared, the young man stood up and was looking eye to eye with Mr. Allbritton.

"Well, young man, what can I do for you?" Mr. Allbritton asked, then said, "Won't you come in the house. We're about to have supper."

When they were in the parlor, Mr. Allbritton turned to see the man better in the light of the coal oil lamp.

"You don't know me, Sir," the young man began to speak. "You see I was born in Three Trails, Oklahoma. My mother was Esther Pearl Brack. Do you remember the name? She named me John and told me that you had a son named John Austin Allbritton. Is that correct?"

"Yes, that was my son, however, he was killed at the Little Big Horn massacre, when he was a private in Custer's 27th Calvary. I haven't heard his name since I buried him at the fort cemetery twenty years ago."

"Yes, sir, he was my father. I never knew him, but Momma had a picture of him and you. He favors you so much I feel that somehow I just had to look you up and get to know my father through you. Momma remarried two years later, and her new husband adopted me. That is the reason my last name is Brack rather than Allbritton." The young man seemed to feel as though he had opened an old wound but continued, "I don't want anything from you. I have a good income and have graduated from high school in Oklahoma. My momma saw to that."

Mr. Allbritton interrupted the fellow, "Nell, my wife, died in childbirth when John Austin was born, so he was raised by an old Indian woman and me. I was in the cavalry and was away on patrol a lot. That's why I needed the Indian woman to help raise my son.

When my son was seventeen, he wanted to join the army. I was very proud of him and his troop. I had no idea that he was or had married your mother. I never knew her, and I am sorry for that."

"No, Sir. They were never married. He and my momma were together the night before he went off to his death. So I never knew him except through the stories Momma told me." John replied.

Mary came into the parlor and announced that supper was ready and that they had better come in and eat.

"Mary, I want to introduce you to my grandson, John Brack," Mr. Allbritton announced. Mary turned pale and gasped, "Your... your grandson?"

"Yes, Mary. He knows too much detail about my son to be anyone else," Mr. Allbritton explained.

"John, let's continue this after supper. I want to know as much as I can about your mother and your past. After all, it isn't everyday a man gets to meet his grandson for the first time." Mr. Allbritton said as he turned and escorted John and Mary into the dinning room.

Before everyone sat down to eat, Mr. Allbritton said he felt that he should give thanks for the new gift which he was presented with this day. After the blessing of the food and the day, they all sat down to eat, except for Mr. Allbritton. The din of the eaters trailed off into silence when they realized he was still standing. With all eyes on him, he spoke in a quivering voice as he began to explain, "I want you all to know that today I have met for the first time my grandson John Brack.

John's mother and my son, John Austin Allbritton, were in love. I don't know if John Austin was afraid to tell me about the young lady or just what reason he had for keeping her a secret. I only know that from their union came my grandson, John Brack. His name was changed because his mother married after John Austin was killed at the Little Big Horn.

Now, this lad has comes to me without any intent except to find me, his grandfather. I will ask each of you to treat him as our family, and I am sure he will return the obligation. This is all I know at this point, but as the time goes on John here will divulge all that he rightly can. God bless you, and now please let's eat this wonderful bounty which God has provided and Mary and the ladies have prepared."

Long after the meal was complete and the dishes were taken from the long table, Mr. Allbritton still sat there staring into his now empty coffee cup. His features never changed until he sighed and sat back in his chair. Looking around, he discovered he was alone at the table.

He rose and went to his favorite chair standing near the fireplace. Picking up his old pipe and packing it with tobacco, he walked out onto the east porch. After scratching a match on the banister, the flame outlined his face in the dark while he pondered the happenings of the day.

He puffed on his pipe and without thinking struck another match and lit the pipe again.

"Is at youngun really yore gran'son, Mista Allbritton?" the question from Earl Ray shocked Mr. Allbritton as he had given no though that someone else was nearby.

"Well, I know that he knows a lot about my son, so I feel that he must be, at least from that standpoint." Mr. Allbritton acknowledged.

John Brack was walking from the stable where he had bedded his stallion down, brushed and fed him. His walk was brisk and intentional as he crossed the ground from the stable to the porch where Mr. Allbritton was smoking his pipe. As John approached the porch, he had a smile on his face and was humming a tune his mother had taught him when he was a small lad.

The evening air was cooler, since the sun had set, and the full moon was just creeping over the scrub. The darkness was set aside for the flickering light of a lantern Mary had just lit and hung on the doorpost of the east porch.

"What strange shadows the scrub casts in the moonlight. I thought I just saw a man in the lane, standing and watching the house," John Brack said as he reached the porch.

"Yeah, that's most likely Ole Chief Billy Bow Legs. Hit's bout time his coffee, salt, and sugar was a runnin out," Earl Ray said as he walked Mary into the house.

John turned back to Mr. Allbritton. "I guess I must be somewhat of a puzzle to you… Mr.… uh what should I call you, Sir? I don't feel that you are comfortable with me calling you grandfather, but Mr. Allbritton sounds so formal, and John, sounds disrespectful. I would like for both of us to be comfortable with each other, and I feel that your speech at the supper table tonight was more than an introduction," John said with pleading in his tone of voice.

"Grandfather is fine. It just takes some getting used to. The only ones who call me grandpa are the twins. They're children of David and Brittany Crocket who live down by the salt pond. Davy is a surveyor and is busy plotting towns in the area. And Brittany, his wife, is the daughter of my old army buddy, Wendell Hampton. I just adore those little boys and, they return my love. So you see I feel like a grandfather to them, yet I feel that you are part of me, too," Mr. Allbritton answered.

"What would you like to know about me? I was born in Oklahoma. After I finished high school, I was a good shot with a rifle and pistol. So the sheriff there in the county gave me a job as a deputy sheriff in the settlement of Three Trails. I was good at what I was doing and soon the sheriff made me the chief deputy over the entire county." John offered eagerly.

"Later I met the U.S marshal from Oklahoma City, and he made me a deputy U.S. marshal. So I wear two badges now, and I may even run for sheriff if the old sheriff doesn't run in the next election. He's tired and getting old. He has slowed down a lot, and I fear for his life."

Mr. Allbritton motioned toward the rocking chairs on the porch, and said, "Let's sit down and we can talk more with our feet up on the rail."

The full moon was up now and shining on Mr. Allbritton's face as he and John talked into the wee hours of the morning. When John Austin's name was mentioned, a tear would sit in his eye, then disappear somewhere on his check.

He was proud of his grandson and was most unhappy to stand and watch him as he rode down the lane toward the north, then round the bend out of sight. Mr. Allbritton continued to stand there and ponder the last few days in his heart. He didn't have anything to leave the lad except his money. If he had wanted that, he never let on that he did.

Were the last few days a dream or did he really meet his own blood grandson, the only kin living? To think, he didn't know about it until this week. Mr. Allbritton sighed, turned, and went into his office.

The full moon was past, and the dark shadows falling around the Bent Penny Cow Pens were somehow different. Yet the scenery was the same.

CHAPTER NINETEEN

CRACKERS AGAINST THE SCRUB FIRE

In the western horizon, the storm clouds gathered as the Florida summer burned on. The afternoon thunderstorms were like clockwork, coming around everyday at the same time. Four o'clock. In the west, distant thunder rolled across the deep blue sky that was over the Bent Penny Cow Pens.

The cattle were especially restless this afternoon, and they bunched in one corner of the cow pen. Each ensuing roll of thunder caused them to move warily to another section of the fence.

Earl Ray was on horseback and rode back and forth along the outside of the split rail fence. He hummed and sang the only song he knew, a lullaby his mother would sing to the children when they were frightened. He sang and hummed as he rode to and fro in order to soothe the cattle inside the pens.

Another distant boom sounded closer this time, a lot closer. Earl Ray sang louder and started to whistle in hopes that Jeremiah, Cliff, Tom, or even John Henry would hear and come out to help keep the cows from stampeding. He sang louder and louder. Although he was terribly out of tune, he kept the song going.

Suddenly, there was a lightning strike just west of the compound. This time, there was no way the cattle were staying inside that fence. They ran in a circle, then straight for the scrub. The rail fence was no match for the frightened cows. The cattle ran as a herd until the next lightning bolt struck in front of them, and they turned and headed directly for Earl Ray.

Earl Ray spurred his horse into a dead run and headed for the stable. He broke out his whip and started cracking it as fast as he could. This was a warning to people in the compound that there was a stampede. He reined his horse up and jumped from the saddle, then did a spread eagle in front of the dinner bell post. Jumping to his feet, he began ringing the bell with all he was worth. At the same time, he watched in horror as the stampeding herd bore down on the corral.

The alert was taken seriously. In moments, hands were running from the stable, bunk house, and the areas around about until the full crew was at hand. They had all heard the cattle running and in moments were on horse back, some riding bareback. They had taken only enough time to slip the bridle on the horse, then were on to the round up.

Another bolt of lightning, and thunder crashed. The herd turned back toward the scrub. This time they disappeared deep into the woods.

There hadn't been a fire in the scrub for many years, so there was a great deal of tinder on the ground, which could fuel a fire and cause serious damage to the scrub and possibly the compound if lightning were to ignite it.

The rain did not follow the lightning but skirted more to the north and left the scrub dry, bone dry. Without the cooling rain, the humidity would double. The heat would be stifling.

It was still about three weeks before the June thunderstorms when Billy Matson drove into the compound with his freight wagon loaded with machinery. The boxes were painted in the familiar green color of *JOHN DEERE*. The crates were unloaded, and the assembly began. There were three, five foot turning plows, an eight foot disc cultivator, and an Acme harrow.

In the meantime, old Will Henry was training the eight mule team to plow with the turning plow. It was hard work because palmetto and oak roots would stop the eight mule team dead in their tracks. There were broken harnesses, plow leads, and even single trees. Chains would not break, yet the power of the mules would bend the hitching curls into straight pieces of iron.

Old Will Henry kept the blacksmith forge going. When something broke, he would mend it or make another piece from whatever was handy. He would hammer it into whatever he needed to repair on the plows.

This June afternoon was going to be a real scorcher. The rain was going around the compound area instead of over it.

Billy Bow Legs rode up and went to the kitchen for a cup of coffee. As he entered, he made the sign of health and fire.

Blossom sat the hot coffee in front of the Indian and made sure the sugar bowl was full, then asked in Seminole what was on fire.

"Not fire yet. Will fire tonight." The Chief's prognostication was not taken lightly, as he could smell the smoke from the fires before the white men could. So he had earned his coffee today.

Mr. Allbritton called Jeremiah and Earl Ray into the office and told them, "You need to post a man on top of the roof of the hay barn tonight and keep watch because the chief says he smells smoke. We don't want to take any chances with fire getting to the compound. The cows can take care of themselves and will probably go to the lakes and wait for the fire to pass. But we can't let it come too close to the Bent Penny or we will be looking for a new place to live."

Three men were assigned to climb the ladder to the top of the hay barn and keep watch. A rope was tied around each. In case they fell asleep, they wouldn't fall off the roof. They took two hour shifts and would keep the cook's triangle to warn everyone if they saw the dreaded glow in the distance.

Around four in the morning, Cliff started up the ladder to spell the man on the roof so he could go get a cup of coffee or use the privy. Just as he stepped onto the second rung the man started ringing the triangle, and shouting, "Fire! Fire! I see the glow in the west. I cain't see no flames yet, but it's gonna be a bigun." Cliff scampered up the ladder and looked toward the west where the glow was rising into the morning darkness.

Cliff told the man, "Go on down and get the other men up and dressed, I see that Mary and Blossom are already in the kitchen. Tell them what we see. Then, go ring the school bell."

Jeremiah, Earl Ray, and the others, including Mr. Allbritton, were headed for the kitchen where they could better talk to the men and assign teams and details for each man.

The dinner bell was rung. Coffee pots were already on the table. Soon breakfast was sitting before the crew.

Mr. Allbritton gravely addressed the men, "Eat hardy! We may not get another hot meal for a while. And while you are eating, I will tell you what you all need to do. First of all, do not panic. There will be a place and time for that when the fire is out. Now the ladies will see that the water barrels are full. When water is used from them, they must be refilled right then. John Henry will be in charge of keeping the barrels full. He will also have buckets of coal oil with torches in case we have to back fire around the compound."

"We will put up a flag to show which way the wind is blowing. If you get caught in the fire, you must not panic but must run fast as you can to the nearest water. Get your clothes wet and stay put until the fire passes you." Mr. Allbritton had taken over the meeting which was a relief to Jeremiah and Earl Ray since they had never experienced a woods or scrub fire.

Davy, Brittany, and the twins came into the dinning hall. Davy immediately went to talk to Mr. Allbritton, Jeremiah, and Earl Ray. Brittany took the twins into the kitchen where they had highchairs. Both sat and watched as their mother started assisting Mary, Blossom and Willie Mae.

"Jeremiah, as you know when we surveyed this township we cut section lines all through the property boundaries. If we work fast we can use those cut lines to act as a fire guard for this property. How many mules can Old Henry hook up to the turning plows? And can he keep the machinery together long enough to plow the fire guards?" Davy was asking and instructing at the same time. The men listened intently to what he had to say. Davy looked around, "Where is Old Will Henry?"

The large black man stood up and said, "I'm rat cheer, Mista Davy. I heared whut y'all said, an I kin hitch all the mules we got harness fer, and they can pull the plows. Cept I hain't shore them hitchin curls'll hold out."

"Well, Will Henry, as soon as you finish your breakfast, why don't you go and start forging as many as you have iron for," Davy ordered.

"Where is Billy Walker?" Davy asked.

Billy's hand shot up, and the ranch hand next to him boosted his eight year old frame on the chair.

"Billy, you are going to have to help Will Henry and keep that forge roaring hot. When he is finished with you, please come to the kitchen and help your mother and the other women. The other men will be needed to fight fire. Now, were depending on you to act as the man here in the house," Davy told Billy, man to man.

"Yes sir!" Billy gloated as this was the first time he had been considered a man to do a man-sized job.

The fingers of smoke announced that the fire was near the boundaries of the Bent Penny compound and closing in on the property.

"Davy hollered to the men, "We want the fire to burn as much of the underbrush as possible, since that will remove the fuel of future fires. Just don't let it get out of control."

The wind, so far, had been favorable to the ranch hands turned fire fighters. The back fires were being set to be carried with the wind.

Will Henry had the mules hitched, and the first fire guard perimeter of the compound dug. His team continued across the pasture to the scrub and the property line. As he approached a section line, he would tie a white rag around a bush to show where he would start next. As the plowing was getting done, the fire blazed closer to the fire guard and the perimeter of the property. The smoke became so bad that he had to shallow set the plows and whip the mules to keep them from running away with the plows.

Other men with axes, machetes, and one and two man saws kept pace with the plows. When the plowing was finished, the disc was hitched to the four-in-hand mule team to smooth out the rough furrows that were plowed around the property. This way the horses could walk or run through the white scrub sand without stepping in a furrow and tipping. The mules worked hard and would drink the water trough dry each time they were led to it.

Old Will Henry was equally dry and would drink several dippers of water each time he came near the house.

The hands were now patrolling the perimeter of the property along the newly disced lane, pulling sleds with water barrels and watching to see that the fire did not jump their lines. If needed, three gunshots would bring the entire crew to keep the fire under control. They would let it burn itself out and then put the hot spots out with shovels, hoes, axes, and water from the barrels.

It took the better part of three weeks for the fire to burn out completely. And then, as though ordered, the rain started to come again each afternoon. The lush grass was turning the blackened scrub green. The cattle could easily be seen no matter where they were because the fire had burned away the underbrush. Now, it was like a fine green meadow that was again coming alive with plants and even the deer and turkeys were returning.

One day, a black bear and her cubs ambled through the compound. The cubs played and sniffed their way the full length of the porch. The sow bear took a drink from the water trough and continued her trek, stopping long enough to call the cubs. They scampered ahead of the mother bear like mischievous children.

The fire was out. The land was growing green. The rains were watering it all and life was again getting back to normal. The cracker cowboys in the scrub had saved the day as well as the ranch. The fire guards were soon overgrown with pasture grass and were now good roads that plied the four directions of the compass throughout the Bent Penny Cow Pens and ranch.

Chapter Twenty

CRACKER SCHOOL HOUSE

Mary Remmick stirred as Earl Ray turned over, sat on the side of the bed, and slipped his pants on. Then he reached for his stockings and pulled them over one foot, then the other. Next, he put his boots on and stood up. For a moment, he yawned as it seemed that four o'clock was coming much too early in the morning. Quietly, he walked over to the door and slowly opened it to avoid the squeak which would finish waking Mary from her sleep.

The door squeaked its objection to the pull of the knob, and Earl Ray muttered to himself, "I jist gotta oil that there ole squeaky hinge." Just outside the dinning hall was the washstand where he washed his face in the fresh, cool water, then put on his shirt.

"Reckon I ought to shave, but heck, I hain't goin no whar. I kin scrape this stuff offen my face in the mawnin." After smoothing the tuft of hair around his head and wetting his bald head with his wet hands, he put on his old straw hat and struck out for the stable to begin his long day's work.

John Henry was already in the barn mucking out the stalls and had already saddled Earl Ray's and Jeremiah's horses. In the meantime, the tackies patiently waited at the hitching rail next to the water trough. Earl

Ray asked, "John Henry, did you git the wood split fer Mary n' the ladies fer the stove?"

"Yes, suh. I done did dat afo four o'clock dis mawnin, an hit been put on the wood box, with fresh kin'lin. Then, I lit out here to git the stables clean, so's I kin go to the school house when Miss Mary go to teachin today," John Henry answered, "Today bees the first day whut me n' Willie Mae kin go to the school."

"Yeah, I'm sure glad I took the schoolin what Mary done give me n' Jeremiah. So's now we kin read, wirte, n' cipher nough to know what we been doin, don cha know." Earl Ray told John Henry.

"How come you hain't got no schoolin afore?" John Henry asked.

"Twernt none back n' Oklahoma where me n' Jeremiah come from. Hit was jist dirt, clay, sand n' cows, I reckon," Earl Ray told John Henry.

Willie Mae walked into the barn and asked John Henry, "Kin you git the eggs for breakfast. We'uns needs bout another dozen?"

"Yassum," John Henry answered, then went on mucking the last stall. He started pitching the waste into a two wheel cart. Might as well take this manure on wid me. I gotta go by the garden no how." Then he pushed the cart from the barn toward the vegetable garden.

The dinner bell rang to get the hired hands to breakfast and start the new day.

John Henry was last to get into breakfast since he was assigned by Willie Mae to pick up the eggs on the way into the kitchen. He placed the eggs on the drain board beside the sink and washed his hands. The pump squeaked and sloshed as he pumped and washed his hands at the same time.

Mary went to the house and started getting ready for her day in school. Willie Mae came in and told Mary, "They's a wagon load o' kids dis morning an they look plum hongry. Kin I give em what's left from breakfast, Miss Mary?"

Mary said, "Of course, Willie Mae, and if you need to make some more pancakes. There's plenty of syrup and butter. They sure work better in school if they had a good meal of a morning."

The children and adults ate everything that Willie Mae and Blossom put out on the table, then went outside and waited until the school bell rang.

While they waited for their teacher, the children were allowed to play tag and other games that they thought up. They were allowed to play in the compound but not around the cow pens or the barns. By the time the school bell rang, the kids were hot and sweaty and in need of a drink of water. Then they found their way into the schoolhouse and their assigned seats.

As she taught the children, the adults were learning, too. On occasion, she would slip in assignments for them, as well. Trying to be a good teacher, she spoke eloquently and disciplined fairly; therefore, her students respected her. Many even adored her. The school day ran well. By noon, the classes were over and the children were loaded up into the wagons and were gone for another day.

Exhausted, Mary told Blossom and Willie Mae that she was going to her room to rest and get the lessons planned for the next day.

John Henry was in the kitchen and asked Willie Mae, "Did you know what Miss Mary a talking bout in the school today?"

"Sure, now go git your chores done and fill up this wood box, too," Willie Mae shouted as she turned and busied herself at the sink. Then she started to sing the A, B,C, song Mary had taught the children. Blossom picked up the tune and started singing with Willie Mae.

John Henry walked down the steps from the kitchen door shaking his head, "I wish hit wuz more easier n'that. I cain't sing, and Willie Mae cain't teach me none. But I jist gotta learn ta read as soon is I kin."

Although there was school daily, any of the hands who wanted to attend were assigned one day a week. The rest of the week was for work at Bent Penny compound. The breakfast meal was also served each morning, and Mary made sure that the children were fed. The adults were always welcome to eat, too.

The school day started with a prayer and the saluting of the flag. Next, they had spelling, then reading. In reading, they mostly learned the alphabet and some sight words. Few books were available. After reading, the children went off to recess. This gave the adults time for closer attention to whatever they needed help on. After recess, came arithmetic and history. Just before school let out Mary would read to the class from the classics or even a newspaper if one happened along.

The adults were pushed through as fast as possible so that they could learn to read and write, count money, and especially sign their name. When they could do that, Mary would give them a test. Then their schooling would be complete. Every time Mary went to Kissimmee; she bought books if there were any available. Once she went to visit the school teacher there who was a pudgy little man with a very bald head. He welcomed Mary and asked what he could do for her. She stated, "Books, we just can't seem to find any good school books for children,"

The school master opened a closet and showed Mary hundreds of books stacked up, also full shelves of books. Some were tattered somewhat but still serviceable in the eyes of Mary.

In awe, Mary struck a deal with the school master to purchase all of them. To haul them home, she went to the general store and had crates put into the wagon. On the way home, she dreamed of the day when her students would be able to read those books. They were her treasures. To display the books, one of the hands built shelves. She had enough books to loan to each child and the adults, too. Those books were a god send to Mary and the children. Now, Mary really felt like she was accomplishing something here at the Bent Penny school house.

CHAPTER TWENTY ONE

CRACKER CATTLE DRIVE

Mr. Allbritton, Jeremiah, Earl Ray, and Mary were in the office discussing the upcoming cattle drive to Tampa. They were sitting around the roll top desk, as Mary made entries into the ledger. She turned to Jeremiah and Earl Ray asking, "How much money will you all need for the drive?"

Mr. Allbritton stirred and shuffled his feet, leaning forward in his chair, and then sat back again.

"Iffen y'all got something to say, Mr. Allbritton, go ahead talk. We'uns want your advice in this here plan, too, don't cha know." Earl Ray spoke and the others nodded agreement.

"When I was driving the cattle to market, I made sure that I had enough gold to pay any of the ranchers that wanted to take their cattle on to my drove. Then, I would settle on a price and pay the rancher in gold. This way, there was no argument as to how much I owed who." Mr. Allbritton spoke. Then he added, "You can take enough gold to buy the supplies you'll need at Fort Blount, then keep the balance of the gold on each of you till you get to where you need it. This way no one will try to steal the gold or even know how much you have on you for the drive."

"That's what we done lass year, too, ain't it? Seems to me, hit worked ᵓood then, too. We'll do er agin," Jeremiah said.

Mary went to the safe and opened the heavy door inside. The strong box lid could no longer be closed because the hold now piled up over the rim of the steal box. There were also bags of gold and stacks of paper money in the pigeon holes of the safe.

Mr. Allbritton looked with astonishment at the trove, and said in a most serious voice, "Why isn't that money in the bank in Kissimmee or Fort Blount? It's okay to have a reserve here at the office but to have tens of thousands of dollars is really dangerous to everyone in this house. Why, people would..." then his voice trailed off as he saw the look of embarrassment on Mary's face.

Mary said, "Well, you see, the banker has taken all he feels he can cover until he gets the insurance from New York for any more deposits form the Bent Penny account."

"I see, but I will still worry until you can deposit that money in the bank." Mr. Allbritton stated. "Anyhow, you will need at least eighty thousand to buy what cattle has been contracted for and to pay the cowhands when we get to Tampa. They will want to blow off a little steam too," he added.

"I figure that we will arrive at Tampa stockyards with about thirty-seven thousand head of cattle," Mary said. Then she asked, "What if we carry some of these bank drafts; then we won't have the weight of all that gold?"

Mr. Allbritton asked, "How much do you think you'll have to draft?"

Mary answered, "We have twenty-one thousand head of cattle here at the Bent Penny Cow Pens. If we pick up the number we have contracted for on the way, we'll need to write at least ten bank drafts. But not all of those ranchers will accept the draft and may want cash or gold. So we need to be sure we have enough of whatever tender we are going to pay out without having to come back to get more money and ride back to the herd. There might be a robbery, and someone could get hurt."

Mr. Allbritton said, "If you are going to add sixteen thousand head to the drive, you will need one hundred and ninety-two thousand dollars, just to pay out the contracts. Do you have that much money in the bank that will cover the drafts for that much of a pay out?"

Mary said, "Yes sir, we can meet that all right."

"Okay. Then, you would be smart to pay as much as you can in the drafts and save the gold to pay off the hands in Tampa." Mr. Allbritton answered.

John Henry and Cliff were stocking the chuck wagon and placing the duffels that the hands brought up to them. In the bottom of the chuck wagon was a false floor where the gold and most of the bank drafts were stashed. The rest of the currency was in the money belts of Jeremiah, Earl Ray, Tom, Cliff, Davy, and Mr. Allbritton.

Willie Mae and Blossom were to drive the chuck wagon while Davy, Will Henry, and Billy Matson joined with three wagon loads of salt. Little Billy proudly rode his new Marsh Tacky Indian pony.

Brittany and the twins stayed with Mary at the cow pens. John Henry and five or six other hands stayed at home base to get things ready for next season.

There were fences to mend; barns and stalls to repair; and four new Marsh Tacky horses to be broken to saddle.

Mary stayed home mainly to teach school because she could not disappoint the neighborhood children.

As many as possible rode on the drive; however, the hands who stayed at home shared in the bounty of the past season's work.

The round up was complete. As the cattle passed single file from the cow pens onto the scrub road heading west toward Tampa, the count reached twenty-two thousand six hundred and fifty-five head.

Mary made note of the count in the ledger, and the drive log sent to Earl Ray who was waiting at the kitchen door. Earl Ray chuckled to himself as he remembered the rock bag counts that he and Jeremiah had used in the early days. They would have needed a lot of rocks today, if not for Mary's ledger.

Before leaving, Earl Ray kissed Mary and took a whole pecan pie out of the pie safe. Carefully mounting his Marsh Tacky, he rode off to catch the head of the herd and the chuck wagon so that he could stash his pie.

When he met up with Jeremiah, he handed him the tally and the drive log and told him what the count was. Jeremiah just nodded his approval.

Driving so many animals through the scrub was hot, slow, dry, dusty, d tiresome. There was little headway because the cattle had to graze as they moved along to the west. Some days they only traveled three or four miles. When they did come to good grazing land, they would stay there for a day or two, and then move on. If the cattle were going trough the scrub, the cowboys would try to keep them in single file so that they could be certain that none of the cows strayed into the brush.

It was late spring, and the quick Florida thunderstorms would come from seemingly nowhere to drench cow and man the same. If there was lightning and thunder, the cowboys had to be especially vigilant. The scrub cattle were accustomed to the thunder and lightning; however, near strikes would often send them stampeding through the scrub and woods. Thus, the constant cracking of the cowboy's whips helped the cattle become accustomed to the sharp cracks. Whether it be the whips or the lightning.

After several days, it had become routine for the hands to catch up with the chuck wagon in time for supper for the day to close.

The horses were picketed, and some were left saddled in case there was a problem during the night that demanded quick response to whatever was happening. Night riders were on two hour shifts. Then they would wake their relief, have a cup of coffee, and turn in for the night.

Breakfast was at four thirty. By five thirty, the cattle were being driven in a big circle to get them back to the west.

The pine woods were clear of underbrush, and the smell of the pines and needles was as fresh as the new day in addition to the aroma of breakfast being cooked which added to the pleasure of greeting the new morning. The crackling of the breakfast fire and the lowing of the cattle echoed among the pines with a stirring beauty of sounds,

Wisps of fog danced among the trees as if a thousand fairies were congregating and entertaining the forest creatures. But soon the sun would come up and expunge the wisps into stark humidity, and the day would be like others until the afternoon showers came to cool the drive for another day.

One day, a deer was shot, and the welcome change of venison for supper was a treat. Blossom made an Indian deer roast, and all the hands ate their fill. Often, they were able to eat potatoes or sweet potatoes, but always the staple was beans.

Another day, the cattle drive came near one of the ranchers who had contracted his cattle to the Bent Penny Cattle Company. As they were passing through the gate single file, Earl Ray sat on the top rail and tallied the rancher's herd.

"One thousand nine hundred and forty-five is the count," Earl Ray said and took the rock bag from the rancher. Jeremiah took the count to Mr. Allbritton who entered it into the log.

"Mr. Jefferson, your count is tallied at twenty-three thousand three hundred and forty dollars." Jeremiah told the rancher. Then he asked, "Will you take a bank draft for that amount?"

"Well Sir, I was a hopin I could git some cash fer them critters." The rancher answered.

"That's fine how much cash will you need before you kin put this here money in the bank?" Jeremiah asked.

"Well, I got to pay off my hands and do some others thangs, I guess I'll take this all in cash," the man said.

Jeremiah went to the wagon and dug out the cash in gold, then handed it to the man and had him make his mark in the log. He asked him if he would like to have a cup of coffee and a piece of pecan pie, but the man declined, thanked them anyhow, and rode off to his ranch in the scrub.

The process repeated itself several more times on the drive, but most of the ranchers would take the draft rather than the un-trusted greenbacks or the bulky gold sacks.

The days turned into weeks, and the weeks became a month. As the out rider came into the camp, he told the group that he could smell salt air about two miles out and felt they were within three days of Tampa.

Mr. Allbritton suggested that Davy take his wagons and go ahead of them to Tampa as they could travel faster than the herd and find out what section of the market they wanted them to drive the herd to.

Davy agreed and the next day the three-wagon train left the herd behind and drove all night in order to arrive in Tampa around eleven o'clock the next day. Davy found the buyer and sent his wagons to the warehouse where the salt was to be stored.

That afternoon, he left to locate the others and found them at the outskirts of the city. He told Jeremiah where to drive the herd, then went back to the warehouse and traded his salt. Surprised at the rate per pound he was paid, he was told that if the salt had been in barrels he would have gotten twice the amount because they were shipping salt to Cuba along with the cattle.

The cattle entered the stockyards, and the count was completed. Mr. Allbritton, Jeremiah, Earl Ray, and Davy went to the buyer to complete the sale.

"Mr. Allbritton, you and the men here brought in forty-one thousand sixty-nine head of cattle. The going price now is thirty-six dollars a head. That brings you one million four hundred seventy-eight thousand four hundred and eighty-four dollars. How do you want the payment? The steamboat captain has that in gold doubloons. However, that's about two and a half tons of gold. Can you carry that amount or would you have him deposit it in the New York Bank here in Tampa?" the buyer offered the group.

"That sounds like a good idea to me, fellows," Mr. Allbritton advised. Then he added, "That much gold will be difficult to transport back to Bent Penny even with Davy's heavy wagons. And we don't have enough strong box capacity to store that money. I think you all should take enough cash or gold to pay off the hands and then put the rest in the bank here in Tampa. Perhaps the deposit limit will be more than at Fort Blount or Kissimmee."

The buyer suggested that he take them over to the Bank of New York and introduce them to the president.

They arrived at the bank and were greeted with a marvelous edifice of marble and granite. Inside the bank were wrought iron bars in front of the teller's cages and a large gate leading to the vault.

The bank president, a very large man in a wool suit, seemed to be the largest man any of them had ever seen. He weighted at least three hundred pounds and stood nearly six foot six. Yet in spite of his mass, he was a very friendly business man and was happy to extol the virtues of his bank. When he was told the amount of the deposit, he turned white and then kind of greenish.

"I uh, I'll have to wire New York if you gentlemen will just excuse me for a few minutes, I'll…" he never finished his sentence as he went out of his office into the teller area. In about ten minutes, he returned with a smile that turned into a grin on his face and announced, "The Bank of New York welcomes you and your deposit. We will be happy to accommodate you with any type of commercial or business account you wish."

After the bank president had finished the transaction, and the gold was safely in his vault, he gave the deposit sheet to Mr. Allbritton and asked them, "May I take you gentlemen to dinner this evening?"

They agreed to go with him as soon as they had paid the hands and seen to the livery of all the horses and mules.

Two of the hands were not found when they gathered the next morning to return to Bent Penny Cow Pens. The fear was that the steamboat captain had shanghaied the pair and that they were on their way to Cuba with the cattle they had just driven to Tampa.

Davy stayed back in Tampa for one more day and found a Cooper who had just moved to Tampa from Kentucky where he had made barrels for the whiskey industry. He had heard that the Florida frontier was going to be the next big "gold rush."

Davy found out that the man was alone and that he had left his family in Kentucky until he could find a town to set up a shop and make barrels. This was exactly who Davy was looking for. When the man heard what Davy was wanting with the barrels, he jumped at the opportunity. Packing up his tools and belongings into one of Davy's wagons, he headed back into the scrub with him.

Homecoming was boisterous and cheerful when Davy arrived with a new member of the Bent Penny business. He, too, was welcomed with open arms.

Phennias Benjamin Cooper was his name, and he was the son to four generations of Coopers who had made barrels for the crown heads of Europe for two hundred years.

Earl Ray went into the kitchen and found Mary busy at the sink. As he turned her around, he handed her a pink ribbon and told her the package was too large to tie up with that little bit of ribbon but he felt she could use the ribbon anyhow. For her school, he had bought ten crates of school books, brand new and never been used. He couldn't have brought her anything better.

Everyone, except the two missing hands, shared in the bonus paid to the hands for a job well done. To further show their appreciation for a job well done, they were going to have barbecue and barn dance next Saturday.

Bent Penny Cow Pens was thriving.

CHAPTER TWENTY TWO

A CRACKER GRAVEYARD

Mary was worried about Mr. Allbritton. For the past week, he had mainly stayed in his room alone. Try as she might, Mary couldn't bring him out of his dolefulness. She had cooked his favorite meals, read his favorite books to him, and tried to get him to respond to her humor and lightness. But there was no light at the end of the tunnel as far as Mr. Allbritton could see.

A certain pallor in his face was evidence of his deterioration. His eyes had begun to sink into his head which caused deeper furrows in the wrinkles around his eyes, the result of many years of squinting in the bright Florida sun. It beat down on him and his cracker cowboy hands as he drove the scrub cows from the woods toward the cow pens all through the long days until sunset. Therefore, he could not open his eyes as a person who was not in the sun all day. It had become a permanent deformation of his face.

After a fortnight of this deep melancholia, Mary found Mr. Allbritton on the front porch of the house looking east toward the cow pens and the pastures which now held another three thousand head of scrub cows and the new hybrid bulls which had been sired by the Texas bull.

To cheer him up, Mary made a warm pot of tea and placed the sugar and cream on the tray along with one of Mr. Allbritton's favorite cigars. With her backside, she pushed the screen door open. In a flourish, she placed the tray on the wicker table beside Mr. Allbritton's rocking chair. Without asking, she poured the brew into his cup and passed the cup and saucer to him. Taking it automatically from her, he lifted the tea to his lips. Still in deep thoughtfulness, he let the cup slip out of his hand and fall once again on the saucer with a delicate clink.

The sound of the teacup hitting the saucer seemed to bring Mr. Allbritton to himself. For the first time, he realized that Mary was sitting beside him.

"Mary, you and the boys are all the family I have. I want you to know that I am extremely proud of the way that Jeremiah and Earl Ray have been running the Bent Penny. They have hired decent hands to help around the house and compound, as well as the cowboys that come around at round up to help with the drove to Tampa. I am glad that you have married and have a life of your own that you don't have to keep this old duffer in line."

Mary interrupted, "It was a labor of love, Mr. Allbritton. I still feel that you are the boss of things around here and that my husband and Jeremiah are still hands. They feel that way, too, and wouldn't change it for the world."

"I know, I know, Mary. That isn't what I'm concerned about. I still wonder if I have taught them everything I can about running a cattle ranch. Yet, they have brought Davy in, and he has the other lines going and the Bent Penny Cattle Company is growing into such a large business. Yet, they know what is happening at any given minute. I feel as though I am a third thumb that is under a very large hammer." Mr. Allbritton concluded.

"That cain't be all that's eatin on you, Mista Allbritton." Earl Ray had arrived without being noticed. "Hit ain't lack we'uns kin do all this without you a sayin yea or nay to whut we's a gonna set out to do. Why, me an Jeremiah would be lost lessen your say so was said."

Mary cringed at the imperfect English which she was trying so hard to help her husband and Jeremiah overcome. However, Mr. Allbritton chuckled at the cracker philosophy that had come from the mouth of his good friend and partner.

"I guess you are right, Earl Ray. Even with you boys and Mary at my side to do for me and my every whim, I still get lonesome. Then I start remembering when Sue Lynn and I roamed these woods. When Becky was born, we were the proudest parents in Florida."

Mr. Allbritton looked out at the cow pens and continued, "We had come from Jacksonville where I had been a colonel in the Army of the United States. Yes, I was a Yankee soldier. When the war ended, I could not get to Philadelphia to find Sue; so I sent for her. Living in a small cottage just outside of Jacksonville on the Saint John's River, I waited for her while fishing a little now and then. One day, I heard what I thought were gun shots behind my house. When I went to investigate, there was a young man wearing a ragged rebel uniform and a straw hat woven out of palmetto leaves. The sound I heard was his whip as he drove about fifteen of the ugliest cows I believe God ever put on the face of this earth. They were skin and bones with long horns. Some had horns that curved inward. All were a brindled color of black and brown with white bellies. The cowboy rode a small horse which was a bit larger than a Shetland, yet smaller than a quarter horse. I was impressed with him and his cur dogs' ability to control these ornery looking cows. When he had come up to the side yard, I hailed him. He stopped but looked at me as if I were going to take his bounty away.

To be friendly, I asked if he would like to use my watering trough and the meadow beside the cottage which would make good grazing for his cattle. He agreed, and I asked him to step down and have a cool drink with me on the porch.

After he gave his dogs a command, they ran over to the herd. Soon, they had the cattle in a circle where they were contented to graze on the lush grass. To my amazement, the dogs never barked, growled, or whined at any time. After introducing myself to the young man, we were soon on the porch watching the sun go down over the Saint John's River. I don't recall his name anymore, but I was so astonished from the tales he told me of the scrub cattle that were everywhere in central Florida and in the south, too. We talked until dark, and then we went inside to get out of the mosquitoes and to get some supper. After eating, he told me about the lakes here about and the woods, scrub, swamps, and hammocks that seemed to be the way all of Florida was when one traveled more than a mile from the city.

He bade me a good night and went to check his herd. The next morning, I didn't hear him leave but I'm sure he first ordered the dogs to move the cattle out. Then, they were on their way to the Jacksonville cow pens where they would load the cattle onto train cars and ship them up north to the market.

When I awoke, I saddled my horse and followed him from a distance to the cow pens. It was a half day's drive from my house. When we reached the collection point, approximately ten to fifteen thousand scrub cows were gathered. Totally amazed, I had no idea there were so many cows anywhere, especially in Florida.

Hooked like a river catfish, I could hardly wait for my wife to get there for us to go find our fame and fortune in scrub cows.

It took about a month for Sue Lynn to get to Jacksonville. By that time, I had talked to every cowboy, buyer, freight yard master, and river boat captain who came and went with cows on board. The money I had to start my business was five hundred dollars for mustering-out pay from the army plus a horse, saddle, repeating rifle and side arms.

To get started laying in supplies for my trek to central Florida, I traded my Yankee army sword for a horse cart. I had cases of ammunition and reloading equipment, a tent, bedrolls, cooking pots and frying pans. I had purchased flour, beans, coffee, tea, water casks, some traps, just in case I wasn't a good forager. When I showed Sue Lynn my list, she made some suggestions which really made our lives on the trail easier and brighter. Something I had forgotten to buy were books to read on the journey."

Mary smiled at this. She shared his love of books.

Mr. Allbritton continued, "On the first day of April 1866, we were off. I had closed up the cottage and told the landlord that we were moving to central Florida. If I had shot him, he would not have been more surprised. He tried to talk us out of going, but our hats were set. After two months of slow travel around lakes, swamps, by bay heads, streams, rivers, and a few friendly Indians, we arrived at this spot, the most beautiful one in all of Florida.

Sue Lynn and I built a lean-to from cypress saplings and palmetto frawns. Soon our camp was visited by two gentle dogs which were possibly lost and glad to find humans with some food. They were thin, old curs, a male and a female. Sue named them Alice and Jerry from an old school book. They liked to work the cows, and we learned a lot from them and the way they would round up cows.

After about a week in camp, the first Indians showed up. The one that was the head man wanted coffee. That was our first meeting with Chief Billy Bow Legs, a grandson of the rebellious Billy Bow Legs of the original Seminole Indian wars. We found he had a sweet tooth, and we soon had to ration the sugar he added to his coffee.

Speaking little English, he would draw and motion well enough to communicate with us.

One day, he was visiting our camp and took us to an old cypress tree where he showed us an English penny nailed to the tree. It had a dent in it where it was apparently struck with a musket ball. Sue Lynn immediately latched onto that scene and started calling this place the Bent Penny Ranch. Well, it stuck and that is the way we came up with such a name for the cow pens.

The Indians helped us build a cabin. Soon we were toasty warm in our new house with dirt floors and felt very fortunate to be out of the weather.

In the spring of 1870, Becky was born. By that time, we were building this house. The sawmill had started up over at Lake Wailes. Since I had plenty of pine and cypress trees on this property, the lumber jacks would cut the wood and haul it to the mill to be sawn. For compensation, I would give them every third tree for their use.

By this time Becky was two years old, we had built this house and most of the barns and other buildings. Also, I was doing well at rounding up cows and driving them to the stockyards in Tampa.

It was on one of these drives as I was coming back from Tampa that one of the Indians came out of the woods motioning me to hurry and follow him. He and I rode hard for a day and a night. When I arrived at the ranch, two Indian women were tending Sue Lynn and Becky because they had contracted malaria and were very feverish," this dark memory caused Mr. Allbritton to pause for a moment. "I was bone-tired from the ride home with the Indian, yet I had to help my family anyway I could.

During that long night as I was sitting and nodding off by Sue Lynn and Becky, I heard what seemed to be voices echoing through the compound. When I got to my senses, Becky had succumbed to the fever. Soon Sue Lynn drew her last breath also. After a day and a night of sitting with them, the Indians took their bodies out to where they had dug two graves. My precious girls were wrapped in blankets and interred under that giant laurel oak just up from the creek. Thankfully, those Indians seemed to know where Sue Lynn would want to be buried because she would sit for hours reading and listening to that creek run by.

Even though I felt like my life and dreams were shattered, I finally came to my senses. The first action I took was to send to Jacksonville for their headstones. When they arrived, I placed them at the head of my two loved ones.

Mary, you came to me as I was on the bottom of the worse times of my life. I wondered what in the world I was doing with a ranch that was hard to tend and a country that was alien and unforgiving. But I knew in my heart that Sue Lynn loved our house and ranch so much that I totally threw myself into it and started to make it pay."

Mary had never been told this sad story before. She leaned in to offer Mr. Allbritton comfort but he was looking into the distance, lost in his life's story.

"While I spent four days in Kissimmee, I met Mary Sykes. Her husband had died and she was working in the general store selling dry goods. I asked her to have supper with me, and she agreed. I told her that I was not looking for a wife that mine had just passed away. However, I truly needed someone to keep house for me, look after the hands, and cook our meals.

Fortunately, she took the job, and I have loved her like a daughter ever since. When she married you, Earl Ray, I was so pleased that she could be happy with another man.

Our old dogs, Alice and Jerry, loved Becky so much that they never left her gravesite no matter how hard I coaxed, and starved themselves to death. We tried to give them anything we thought they would eat but they wouldn't eat or drink. I buried them next to Becky and was glad that before her death, Alice had given birth to six pups which were weaned before their parents grieved to death.

For a time, I've wanted you all to know how the little graveyard got there and who was buried there, also how the ranch got its name. I think that Mary has been writing most of the daily events in her diary, so she can now tie all this in with what you already know." Mr. Allbritton sat back in his rocker taking a long pull from the cigar which Mary had added to the tea tray. He took another sip from the cup and placed it carefully in the saucer. Then he said, "I'm tired now. I think I will go in and go to bed. God bless you and I will see you bright and early in the morning."

CHAPTER TWENTY THREE

A CRACKER CHURCH SERMON

Sunday morning in the scrub was pretty much like any other day at the Bent Penny Ranch. Before church, the same old chores had to be finished: as usual pens require checking in case any calves were born overnight, then they were separated from the herd. The horses, chickens, hogs, dogs and cats had to be fed. And only then could they think of themselves and take the time to get dressed for the church meeting.

On Sundays, the school was used for church meetings; and families from the surrounding areas traveled to Bent Penny School to attend the services. Usually Mr. Allbritton led the time of worship having Mary read the Bible, then explaining what the text meant and how to apply it in their daily lives. He was a very good speaker and was steeped in knowledge of the *King James Bible*. His experiences in life and the sacrifices he had made had given him the wisdom, humility, earnestness, and humor to be a wonderful lay preacher.

On this particular Sunday morning, the church was packed, as usual. Mr. Allbritton was sitting on the seat in the front row and was contemplating the American flag with two new stars which represented the twenty-eighth state of Iowa and Florida, the twenty-seventh.

With his head bowed, he thought about the men who had perpetrated crimes against the ranch, the horses, and cattle; even rustling Indian's livestock. He thought about how the government had put a price on some of those men's heads and what a shame it was that money would be paid for the capture or killing of a man. He knew the punishment must fit the crime however; the whole country and society would be shaped only by nihilism. Terror is never comfortable for any soul in the world.

Dictators and obtuse rulers had tried in the past. The public had finally revolted against the lawlessness and would always bring the Judeo-Christian morals back into the leadership until the next fellow came along telling the people what they wanted to hear. All the while he was plotting a way to become the next dictator.

Mr. Allbritton shook off those negative thoughts yet took from them the high points and noted them on the margin of his written sermon.

While Mary pumped and played the organ, Mr. Allbritton led the singing. After the songs were sung, he stood there on the podium and looked out at the faces of the people who were gathered in the small, cramped schoolhouse.

Men, fathers, mothers, children, young, and old all sat in rapt attention as they anticipated the morning's sermon.

The prayer Mr. Allbritton prayed was short and to the point. It had been from the wedding ritual, "What we see that God has put together, let no man put asunder. Amen."

"I know most of you folks personally and a lot of you by name. I know all of you by your faith, and I certainly am happy to have you come up to me and shake my hand. Not one of you would rob me or try to cheat or steal from me. Yet, you are taking something from me every week, and I am not getting any of it back. You are not stealing this, for I have given it to you of my own free will. And, honestly and truthfully, it is yours to keep. But, I cannot tell if you are practicing what I preach to you on Sunday. If there is trouble, you are welcome to come to me; we will try to solve the problem. If you are lonesome, you are welcome to come for a visit and just talk. If your problem is financial, we as a church will try to see that your needs are met. Neither the church nor I will turn you away, nor will we judge you. Your fate and judgment are up to God's grace and mercy which you need to travel in His team. Jesus said that the way is difficult and that the yoke is heavy, but He was stating this to point out how these things are if you don't believe in Him.

We have most recently become the twenty-seventh state in the Union. With this, we have a greater obligation to each other than to the state of Florida, or Polk County. We are the government just as we are the church. The building is not the church, but those souls which make up the congregation are the church." Mr. Allbritton paused, wiped the sweat from his brow with his red bandana, took a sip of water from the glass on the table, and continued with his sermon.

As he was finishing his sermon, he told the congregation that there was a basket by the door which was a special offering for a needy family near the settlement at Lake Wailes. If they could, donate, he promised that Bent Penny ranch would match whatever they gave.

"And don't forget we are having dinner here on the grounds today to enjoy each other in fellowship."

Mr. Allbritton wiped the sweat from his brow again and sat down.

Mary played the organ as everyone filed out of the building. Outside, the bell in the tower was ringing to signal the hands to come and enjoy the weekly feast and fellowship.

As they gathered, no one noticed Mr. Allbritton walking slowly down the stairs and clutching tightly to the railing. As he staggered toward the house, Mary looked up to see him going into the kitchen.

"That's strange," she said to herself. "He usually goes directly into his office. Maybe he just wants another cup of coffee."

As usual, the feast turned into a festival as the men showed off their prowess with the cracker cow whip, lasso or simply arm wrestling. The ladies showed off their new bonnets or dresses which they had made for the services. Then, as the day turned into early evening, guitars, fiddles, and other musical instruments appeared. People began singing their favorite songs and hymns. Often, the brightness of a full moon lighted their way as the members reluctantly tightened the cinches on their saddles and hitched up the wagons, and buggies for the trip back home and to the new week in front of them.

Mary took the basket from the table beside the door and carried it to the office to count the money.

As she entered, she noticed Mr. Allbritton sitting at the roll top desk. Quietly, he mumbled, "Sue Lynn," then fell to the floor.

As Mary screamed, Jeremiah rushed into the room, followed by Earl Ray and Davy. Urgently picking Mr. Allbritton up, they carried him to his room where the men undressed him and put him in his bed.

"Who's a ridin night guard?" Earl Ray asked.

Jeremiah answered, "I think Tom aire."

"Send him to the Injuns an git that there ole woman and send Cliff to Fort Blount an git that doc. He's to take the buggy and I mean whomp that there horse to a lather a gittin' there." Earl Ray ordered.

Mary poured a small sip of brandy and put it to Mr. Allbritton's lips, but he turned his head away and said, "I don't want to go to my maker with booze on my breath." She handed the jigger to John Henry Luke. Taking it, he looked around, shrugged his shoulders, and drank the dram down. Then he placed the glass on the table beside the open bottle.

Willie Mae poked John Henry in the side, gave him a dirty look, then picked up the small glass, and went back to the kitchen.

In about an hour, the Indian woman came into the room and looked at Mr. Allbritton. After taking his pulse, she pulled his bottom eyelid down peering into the eye. Then she let the eyelid go back into place and watched it stay open. Sadly gazing at Mary, she tenderly closed his eye.

The Indian woman said one word, "Tuombe," then added, "You say stroke."

The word hit Mary like a four foot split rail, and she dashed out of the room sobbing. Finding herself in the barn, she stood beside Tacky, Mr. Allbritton's favorite Marsh Tacky horse and wept with deep sobs. Even though Earl Ray stood beside her with tears in his eyes and his arm around her, she felt no consolation. Deep, deep grief enveloped.

It was just sunup when Cliff raced into the yard and pulled the white team of horses up in front of the door. He helped the doctor down and led him to where Mr. Allbritton was lying.

John Henry led the horses and buggy to the barn, unhitched the buggy, and walked the horses around the coral until they were cool enough to curry dry. After that, he watched them and gave them an extra ration of oats before returning to the house.

John Henry went to the kitchen where Willie Mae was busy boiling water and making coffee. She fried bacon and eggs and had biscuits in the oven, but she suspected that no one would be hungry this morning. John took Willie Mae by the arm and led her over to one of the benches beneath the long table. Without speaking, he kneeled down. Willie Mae followed suit, and they prayed openly for the life of their best friend in the entire world.

The doctor finished his examination of Mr. Allbritton, then turning said, "Where can I get a cup of coffee around here?"

Mary took him by the arm and led him into the kitchen where Willie Mae and John Henry were still deep in prayer. Mary started to interrupt but the doctor told her. "No, no, he'll need all of that he can get." Then he looked into the faces of the people who had gathered in the kitchen. Just about all the hands and many friends were now packed in there.

The crowd instantly hushed, so the doctor spoke to them: "Mr. Allbritton has suffered a stroke. At this time, I cannot tell the extent of the damage; however, if you will keep his head flat and him quiet, we will know in two or three days. First, he will try to move. The side that doesn't move is the side the stroke is on. We can only hope that it happened to the left side of the brain. If it is the right side, that affects the speech, for some reason. So, if he can move his left arm, leg, or eyelid, he will be able to talk soon. If not, you will have communicated with him for the last time." The doctor turned away and asked, "Now where is that coffee?"

Since Willie Mae and John Henry had finished praying, she handed the doctor a cup with piping hot coffee, then asked, "Mista Doctah, you want cream n' sugar fo dat?"

"No, no thank you. I'll just drink it black." The doctor said. He looked at a thousand questions on the faces of the people in the dining hall and waited until the words would form in their minds so that they could ask the question that was on their face.

The doctor sat down at one end of the long table, and Willie Mae set a sumptuous breakfast before him. He looked into her face and saw a tear fall from her cheek, just missing his coffee cup and landing on the clean tablecloth. He smiled up at her and nodded his acceptance of her silent apology.

Days and nights seemed to run together there. For a long while, Mr. Allbritton did not speak nor move except when the men would roll him over to change the sheets on the bed or to keep him from getting bed sores.

Mary did not leave his bedside except to use the outhouse or eat a quick snack. Willie Mae kept a glass of cool water beside her and would bring her a cup of coffee when she thought Mary would like to take a short break.

It was midnight of the fourth day when Mary heard the sheets rustle. She quickly stood over Mr. Allbritton who was looking up at her and asked, "What does a man have to do to get something to eat around here?"

Mary answered through tears and laughter, "You just said the magic word. Breakfast will be right up." And for the first time since Sunday night, she left his bedside and ran the twenty yards or so to pound on Willie Mae and John Henry's door.

John Henry answered the knock. When he saw that it was Mary, he shouted, "Mae git up! Miz Mary be here." Then quickly, he asked, "Whut's wrong, Miz Mary? Is Mista Allbritton..." his question trailed off, and Mary took up the news.

"He's awake and hungry."

John Henry closed the door, but it opened again immediately. Willie Mae rushed out and ran to the kitchen. By the time John Henry got his clothes on and to the kitchen, Willie Mae had a roaring fire going in the wood stove.

Two eggs, two slices of bacon, two biscuits, and a serving of grits with butter, fresh strawberry jam, and hot coffee was on the tray and set before Mr. Allbritton within the span of an hour.

The doctor arrived later that morning. When he saw the patient, he smiled and said, "Well I don't think that your stroke was as bad as I thought it was. You seem to have some weakness in the left side, but I would say you will have a full recovery if you will do as I say." He took off his glasses and started to wipe them with his kerchief. Looking at Mary, he began, "Now you are my witness, and I expect you to follow this advice to the letter. First, he must not smoke any tobacco products. He must not get up from his bed for another week and then only to go to the kitchen for meals and to the porch for fresh air. No horseback riding and very little buggy riding. Someone must be with him for twenty-four hours a day until he can ambulate on his own." Looking at Mr. Allbritton, he lectured, "You will know when that is, for the room and world will no longer spin in front of you as it is now. You may have a regular diet but watch out. Don't gain too much weight. Sometimes your appetite will be as good as when you were punching cows all day, but you won't be, so don't eat like you were."

The doctor finished by asking, "Do you have any questions? Now am I too late for breakfast or too early for dinner? I am hungry and I really need a cup of Willie Mae's coffee." He ate a hearty breakfast, then stepped into his buggy, and headed north toward Fort Cummins.

CHAPTER TWENTY FOUR

CRACKER ANGELS

Mr. Allbritton had begun to recover from his stroke. Little by little, he was enjoying visitors from around the area. Some of the folks who brought their children to school stopped by and wished him a speedy recovery. They would often stay until Mary stepped out on the porch where Mr. Allbritton was enjoying the visitors. With a clear "Ahem!" she would clear the way for him to rest or take a dose of medicine.

There were no visitor that thrilled the invalid more than the Pierce twins, Davy and Johnny. When they were on the porch with Mr. Allbritton, the aura was bright around him. Gleefully, he laughed and joked with the boys as they romped and ran around him and his rocking chair. He would hold them in his lap telling them stories about the old days which kept them spellbound with stories of *Uncle Remuis* and the Tar Baby or Brer Fox always failing to capture Brer Rabbit.

Little Billy would come over, and the three boys would play around the house until the shouting and yelling got on Brittany's and Orange Blossom's nerves. Then one or the other would go and grab the boys by their arms, march them to the porch, and sit them on the floor in front of Mr. Allbritton. Immediately afterwards, they were served warm tea with sugar and milk; cookies or short cakes would round out the snack time. This would give the adults a respite from the ever energized children and not wear Mr. Allbritton down; however he always enjoyed the boys and knew that the whooping and hollering was a part of them.

All the children around the Bent Penny called Mr. Allbritton, Uncle John, which really pleased the old man. He would laugh and retell the tales about the cute saying of the boys as well as the mispronounced words which made him chuckle again and again.

One afternoon after Little Billy was released from school, he raced across the pasture to play with Davy and Johnny and found them playing near the creek. As he approached, Davy fell into the stream and started splashing in the waist deep water. Billy ran over, jumped into the creek and pulled Davy to the edge. Johnny had already run to the house, calling his mama to come and help Little Billy. By this time, the seven year-old Billy had the lad on the bank and was slapping Davy on the back to make him cough out the water he had swallowed.

Brittany ran to the creek, scooped up her charge, and continued back to the house where she dried him off and calmed him down.

For days, his scare was the topic of the compound, and Mr. Allbritton teased Davy about his swimming lessons.

Little Billy made sure that when the story was repeated in his presence he would say, "I jumped in and saved Davy's life, Uncle John. He wasn't trying to learn how to swim," never fully understanding Mr. Allbritton's humor.

One of the lessons Mary taught in the school was music and the children were singing as Mr. Allbritton was sitting on the porch. The strains of familiar songs were settling on his ears, so he began to hum the tune, also. Soon he was deep in thought and did not hear the school bell peal signaling the end of the school day until three rambunctious boys broke his reverie like a dropped water melon. And these sweet pieces were his 'dopted grand children.

Tom and Blossom's baby girl was now almost three years old and was the apple of her Uncle John's eye. Mary "R", as she was called, would come up to Mr. Allbritton holding her arms up causing him to pull her up on his lap. He would sing to her, and she would often fall asleep while listening to his deep, soothing voice.

Seldom were there times when Mr. Allbritton was totally alone any more. It seemed that someone from the school or ranch, and nearly always the children, which Mr. Allbritton called his cracker angels, were at his side or on his lap. He simply reveled in the feeling of being of one spirit with the people and children of the ranch.

Usually when supper was ready, he would take one or two children by the hand, lead them to the table, and seat them on each side of him. As the supper was served, he would act as if he were going to eat their meal, too. This prevented any picky eaters at the meal.

One evening, Mary R was sitting by him when she began to whimper. When Mr. Allbritton asked what was wrong with her, she answered "I no got toffee, too. Uncle John gots toffee. Me wants toffee like Uncle John," He took his teaspoon and dipped a spoonful of coffee from his cup and put it into her glass of milk. She immediately took a drink of her milk, smacked her lips, and said, "Good fwesh gown toffee!" Everyone at the table laughed and went on to enjoy the meal.

The toll of all the constant visitors had began to show on Mr. Allbritton's face. The lines deepened, and he was losing the color which had stained his face and hands from the skin tanning effect of the Florida sun. His bushy mustache needed trimming as he did not shave himself any more, which made his face seem even smaller. His eyes had begun to set back in his head again, and Mary worried that he was again slipping into a stroke.

The next day he asked Mary if he could take a drive over to the salt pond and talk to Brittany while the children were in school. Mary called John Henry and asked him to hitch the buggy and drive Mr. Allbritton over to Davy and Brittany's.

The buggy was a comfortable way for Mr. Allbritton to get around. He could drive himself, but Mary would have none of it, and asked John Henry to take him everywhere he wanted to go. This morning was a very fine day. As he rode toward the salt pond, he listened to the birds singing and the crows squawking. A mocking bird sang her song and followed up with a chirp that seemed to end that particular song. Blue jays frolicked along the tree limbs, and a gopher tortoise walked by slowly and deliberately into the path of the buggy. Mr. Allbritton asked

John Henry to pull up and let the animal pass. He patiently watched it as it crossed the road and disappeared into the scrub.

Brittany was babysitting Mary R for Blossom and had put her down for a nap when the buggy drove into the yard.

Brittany came out to the side of the buggy and gave Mr. Allbritton a big hug. She told him to come into the house. As they entered, Mr. Allbritton asked. "Where's Mary R? Is she sleeping?" Brittany told him that she was and so he kept his voice down to a loud whisper.

He chatted with Brittany for the best part of an hour, and then said, "Well, I must be going now and please give Mary R, a big hug for me."

Mr. Allbritton stepped into the buggy, and John Henry rapped the reins on the horses' rump and away they went back toward the house. As the buggy passed the school, the strains of *Nearer My God to Thee*, floated across the compound and in the ears of anyone within ear shot of the school. Mr. Allbritton asked John Henry if he would whoa up in front of the school so he could hear the children singing.

After a while, the children finished singing, John Henry turned toward Mr. Allbritton who had slumped over in the seat. His face was as blue as ink, and he had ceased to breath. Mr. Allbritton had gone to the Lord while listening to his precious cracker angels.

CHAPTER TWENTY FIVE

A CRAKER FAREWELL

Jeremiah and Earl Ray carried Mr. Allbritton's lifeless body into the house and lay him on a table which Mary had spread a bright, clean white sheet over. His head rested on a souvenir, satin cushion he had brought home from his trip to Savannah, Georgia. The golden tassel around the fringe of the pillow outlined his sliver hair which would reach below his collar if he were standing. This was usually the way the cracker men wore their hair in back to keep the blazing sun from burning their neck. Mosquitoes and biting flies were also eliminated with the long mane.

The long hair seemed not to have been much help to the back of Mr. Allbritton's neck because it was like tough leather, and the wrinkles in his face still gave the illusion of a permanent smile.

Mary hung quilts on ropes to screen the body and give privacy to the ordeal which Jeremiah and Earl Ray felt was their duty to Mr. Allbritton. It was in loyal love that they undressed and washed him with warm water and soap. After that, they dressed him in his best black, wool suit which Mary, Willie Mae, and Orange Blossom had spent much time brushing and pressing. A light blue kerchief was tied loosely around this neck and tucked inside the collar of his white, starched Sunday shirt. His boots were polished and shone like never before. John Henry had spent extra time shining the boots because he knew it was the last time he would ever polish boots for such a great man as this.

While the body was being prepared, Tom Walker and Cliff Teague brought Mr. Allbritton's bed into the front room of the house where Mary and Willie Mae made the bed with clean fresh sheets and a fine spread of Mary's; which was a part of her trousseau.

When Jeremiah and Earl Ray had finished grooming and dressing his body, they placed him gently on his bed, folded his hands, and then covered him up to his chest. The souvenir pillow was placed once more under his head.

Orange Blossom went outdoors and was gone overnight until morning when she was again in the kitchen starting the fire in the stove. When Willie Mae came she was surprised to see Blossom busy getting things ready for the breakfast meal.

"War y'all been at all night? Don't choo know Mista Tom done been worried sick cause you ain't home to tend your babies?" Willie Mae scolded Blossom.

Blossom's face reddened, then paled as she realized that Willie Mae was also worried about her whereabouts' during the night.

Her questions were answered when Chief Billy Bow Legs walked into the kitchen and sat down in a chair. His countenance was very grim. Often while he spoke to Blossom in Seminole, a tear would give away his sadness and passion for his friend. It was very unusual for an Indian to weep; however, when such a good friend dies, there is nothing to keep back his tears.

About that time, Willie Mae saw a large fire in the middle of the compound and ran to the door to see what was happening. Blossom took her by the arm to stop her rush. That's when Willie Mae saw the rest of the chief's party sitting in silence around the great fire.

The news of the death of Mr. Allbritton spread through the scrub like lightning fire. Soon people from as far away as Kissimmee, Fort Blount and Fort Cummins came to pay their respect to the patriarch of the Bent Penny Cow Pens.

The undertaker from Kissimmee had driven out to the ranch to offer his services and brought with him the coffin which Mr. Allbritton had picked out some months before, during one of his trips to town.

The coffin was simple cypress and pine with polished brass bars on both sides. The wood was sanded and varnished like fine furniture with an inside lined in satin and a monogram J B A. No one had ever seen or heard of a middle name for Mr. Allbritton, and it wasn't until later that the mystery was solved. The casket was large but not overpowering. The beauty of the fine craftsmanship was awesome to see and a fitting resting place for this wonderful man.

Wendell and Mary Ellen Hampton arrived just two days after the death of their good friend. With them present at the ranch, the funeral plans were complete.

Mr. Allbritton's body was laid in the casket. The pall was two saw horses in the front room draped with white sheets. When the doors were opened, people began to file past the bier. Silent sobs were heard as Mary, Jeremiah, and Earl Ray stood at the head of his coffin to shake hands with the now hundreds of people who passed by the casket.

Mary thought, "How on earth am I or we going to feed all these people?" as it was the custom to feed all who came to visit or pay their respects. Most of the people were not even thinking along those lines, but Mary certainly was.

The visitors signed the book. If they only made their mark, Orange Blossom who could now write, wrote their name beside the mark. Even the Seminoles passed by the coffin but would not look into the face of the dead man.

When all had paid their respects to the deceased, they waited in two lines outside the door where the undertaker had parked his horse drawn hearse.

Jeremiah, Earl Ray, John Henry, Davy, Tom, and Cliff were the pall bearers. As they carried the casket it seemed to float out the door and down the steps to the back of the hearse. The coffin was rolled into the hearse and locked in place. Mr. Allbritton's Marsh Tacky horse was tied to the rear of the hearse with its head lower than usual as if he knew he would never feel the tender touch of his master and rider again. Mr. Allbritton's riding boots were turned backward in the stirrups, and his black riding frock was draped over the saddle.

Stepping up to the seat, the undertaker flipped the reins, causing the snowy white horses to step out, as the black plumes which were fastened to the horses' collars fluttered in the breeze. As the hearse passed, the men would remove their hats and the women would bow their heads and curtsey. Afterwards, they would fall into line to march down the trail to the cemetery in the scrub where he would be placed beside his loved ones who were indeed with him on this day.

The eulogy was given by Wendell Hampton, his old and good friend from the days in the Yankee Army. And the praise heaped on the mountain of a man was punctuated by amen's from the crowd around the graves. For the first time, the name John Brokenbow Allbritton was made known to all who were there. Now they knew what the "B" in the monogram stood for.

The grave was closed by the hands, each having a turn at the shovels. Soon, the grave was covered with beautiful wild flowers which included the Florida orchid, magnolias, and other plants from the scrub and bay head near by.

After most of the people had left the site, Mary, Jeremiah, and Earl Ray tarried beside the grave and wept as they remembered the few short years they had known Mr. Allbritton and his kindness and generosity to them all.

As they returned to the compound, people were eating and drinking lemonade which the ladies made from the rough Florida wild lemons. It turned out that the Indians had brought and prepared venison, turkey, and wild hogs. There were even sweet potatoes, pinto beans, cornbread, and lots and lots of pies and cakes. Each family had brought food which they had prepared at home and shared with everyone else who was there.

After the meal, the Seminole Indians walked into the scrub. Shortly, there came plaintive cries from the gravesite as the Indians were holding their own Seminole send-off of their friend and benefactor of many years. Now they felt an uncertainty, which was a moot point as long as Mary was alive and still part of the Bent Penny Ranch and Cattle Company.

Chapter Twenty Six

CRACKERS RETURN TO THE SCRUB

Sundown and in the minimum of twilight in the scrub, the mourners lit lanterns and hung them beside the wagon or other vehicle which had conveyed them to the Bent Penny Ranch and Mr. Allbritton's funeral. They had begun to drift back into the scrub and home. There was a silence which was felt more than heard as they traveled, each in their own way. Some spoke quietly as if still in the midst of the rites; others were totally silent and were as buried in their thoughts as much as the lifeless body they had come to bury.

Jeremiah and Earl Ray stood beside the grave with their whips and began cracking them in final honor of their fallen mentor, teacher, and great friend. The cracks numbered one hundred in all, and then ceased. Again silence. The scrub absorbed the sound just as it would the remains of this great man.

The coiled whips were hung on the rack in the hallway with their hats; however, Mr. Allbritton's hat and whip were never moved or touched again, in his honor. Willie Mae and Orange Blossom kept them dusted and never took them down.

As things began to return to some frame of normalcy, the ever present vacuum of the lack of a guiding hand and soft suggestion was the silence that screamed in their ears as they went about the daily routine and chores. The women were often caught with tears welling in their eyes and aprons, dabbing tears away. The men just bucked up a little more.

Now the round up was welcome as it took their minds off the new grave in the little cemetery in the hammock.

"They's less then twenty thousand head this here year." Jeremiah told Earl Ray and Mary as they were seated in the office, mapping out the plans for the up-coming drive to Tampa.

"We's in the office Davy." Jeremiah shouted through the screen door. As Davy opened the door and walked in the office, Earl Ray commented. "Your ears musta been a burnin sumpin tragic, cuz we wuz jist talking bout choo, Davy."

"Yep, we wuz, Davy, fer a fact. We'uns was a thanking you and Brittany an the twins might lack to stay in Tamper fer a spell whilest me'n Earl Ray droves the lass o' them cow critter to the stockyard in Tamper." Jeremiah declared, as he poured a cup of coffee from the coffee pot that Willie Mae had just brought in and set on the table in front of meeting quartet.

"Why yes. Funny you should mention that. I came to see if you all minded if we went to Tampa to check on the warehouse that is to store the salt that's going to be shipped as soon as we can supply a ship load. We already have that much. But with the funeral and all, we got a little behind in the harvesting and barreling." Davy sipped his coffee then added, "That would fit in just fine and Brittany and the boys could see the sights of the big city. Brittany especially wants to go to the theater and for the first time in several years get all dressed up and do the town with dinner, theater, and dancing. We would like to take Orange Blossom and her children, too, so the twins would have familiar company to play with and Blossom could sit with the children while Brittany and I are seeing the town."

Mary spoke up and said. "I just might go and see that you two don't get too caught up in the merriment of the big city. Besides Earl Ray and I haven't had any time for ourselves in several years. So, maybe it's time for the old married folks to kick up their heels, too!"

Earl Ray looked at Mary and asked, "Whar you thank I'm a gonna git all that that energy from? I hain't no spring cowboy who kin go out a hootin and holler'n all night and round up cow critters in the day. I hain't got that much git up an go no more lack I usta do."

Mary laughed. And it seemed almost sacrilegious. It was the first time she really felt like laughing since the funeral. But she let herself go and laughed and chided Earl Ray comparing him to the Texas bull in the corral.

Earl Ray blushed scuffling his feet on the floor, then looked at Mary and retorted, "Yeah, thar is thangs I kin do, and thar aire things I cain't do. We'uns 'll find out what's which when we'un come to town."

On a cool May morning, the first chuck wagon led off before dawn. In the meantime, the two dirt ruts had given way to a clay road that snaked its way through the scrub. In some cases, there were settlements springing up along the road; which was now known as the Bent Penny Trace. As it entered Fort Blount, now known as Bartow which was the seat of Polk County government, the trace became red brick pavers; and the wagons and cows made noisy procession through the city.

The men riding drag (usually the newest hired) had to clean up the manure that was left by the uncaring herd. A manure wagon was the last vehicle in procession. And with shovels and brooms, every scrap was removed with swift dispatch to be hauled to the nearest house who wanted the natural fertilizer for the garden or roses. The odor of the herd lingered for several days or until the first cleansing rain. Then, the streets were ready once again for the political gentry to trod upon.

As the drive from the Bent Penny Ranch to the stockyards in Tampa took a long three weeks, the second herd of the total drove was being readied. First they were dipped and placed in the drying pasture where they stayed overnight. Then, they were moved to the feeding pens to be fed hay and plenty of salt and water. A windmill pumped water, day and night, to keep the troughs full. As they gained weight, the cattle were left to eat and graze to their content. Later, they were walked, at their own speed to stock yards so they wouldn't lose weight on the trip. That took a lot of time and patience for the cracker cowboys as they moseyed along at the slow pace of the cattle while they kept them bunched and steadily moving toward their fate in Tampa.

As the herd neared the Fort Lonesome cut off, Davy came galloping up with his horse in a lather.

Jeremiah spurred up his little Marsh Tacky to meet him.

"Jeremiah, the price has fallen at the Tampa stockyards and there is virtually no market for the cows in the north since the tick scare. Now, you can turn and take them to Punta Rassa or Fort Myers, where the market is still strong going into Cuba. But you need to keep them moving even if you do run a few pounds off them, for they will be driving everything from Tampa to the pens in the south." Davy was almost shouting.

Jeremiah turned and was walking his horse back toward the herd while making his decision.

"Davy, kin you manage the herd fer a few days? I thank I'll ride back to the ranch and tell Earl Ray to take the south fork to Fote Mars and let this here herd turn south from here to Fote Lonesome to the trail. Ya'll mos lackly be meeting the second herd at the Caloosahatchee trail to Puna Rassa. We'll lackly hafta swim this herd cross the river but Earl Ray kin brang tha res round the south to Fote Mars. I thank Punta Rassa is a gonna fill up to fas' fer us'ens to git thar in time. So we gonna jist by pass that thar un this time."

Davy agreed, and Jeremiah left his first herd behind as he galloped his little horse toward the ranch.

It took Jeremiah most of a day to get back to the ranch and tell Earl Ray and Mary what had happened in the Tampa market.

Then he went to the schoolhouse and rang the bell. Since it was almost dark, all the hands came out to see what was going on in the compound. As Jeremiah and Earl Ray stood at the top of the steps and waved their hands, the cracker cowboys came close so that they all could hear.

Fellers we'uns needs to change the plan a mite. We'uns gotta git to Fote Mars before the market drops fer the cows critters sail to Cuba. That mean we'uns is gotta git a movin as soon as everybody has et. So go now and git your grub, then saddle up and start a circle'n them critters and move them out as soon as you kin. We'uns 'll hafta worry bout strays when we gits back from the drove," Jeremiah spoke to the men with authority and directed the straw bosses to make sure that their team kept the cattle moving day and night. The chuck wagons were dispatched in two hours and told to get ten miles away before stopping to cook breakfast for the men. Then, as soon as the last man was fed, they should clean up and overtake the herd, then set up ten miles ahead for the next meal.

Mary and Charlie, the black smith, were the only ones left when the last of the cracker cowboys disappeared down the Bent Penny Trace.

Day in and day out the anvil rang from the blows of the hammer as the blacksmith's forge flamed and sparks flew while he was hammering and hammering on the wrought iron.

Mary was too preoccupied to really notice that the hammering had stopped and the smithy's forge was no longer belching out smoke and sparks.

She did notice a mule and a flatbed wagon moving along the trail toward the salt pond but did not give it much thought. Continuing to work in the office until it was time for her to start a meal; she went to the large empty kitchen and fired up the wood stove to prepare the meal for her and Charlie.

This noon, though, Charlie didn't show up to eat, so she just thought that perhaps he had to finish a project before the men got back home.

That evening, Charlie came to the kitchen and sat at the table nearest the stove where Mary was busy with the supper meal. She poured him a cup of coffee and he took the sugar and milk to cool if off so that he could drink the tan liquid. As he touched the cup to his lips, he sat it back on the table and asked. "Miz Mary…. Do u'en thank Mista Earl Ray'll come mad on me iffen I done sumpin he hain't said I kin do, you reckon?"

Mary looked quizzically at the blacksmith and said, "Why Charlie, what have you don that is so bad?"

"Hit ain't bad Miz Mary, least I thank hit ain't so much. Hit be jist sumpin I was a hankerin' ta do, and I a done did hit." Charlie replied.

Mary said, "Well what is it Charlie?"

"Mebby I otter show ye afta breakfast in the mawnin I'll take you and let you see hit fer yoreself." Charlie replied thoughtfully.

At sunup, the buggy was hitched and tied at the rail in front of the office, waiting for breakfast to be finished so they could go see the project that the smithy had been working on so diligently for the past few days.

Charlie helped Mary into the buggy and went around and climbed in the other side, took the reins, slapped them on the horse's rump, and commanded. "Git up!" Soon they were approaching the cemetery, and

Mary immediately noticed the black wrought iron picket fence around the entire graveyard. She gasped and tears began to cascade down her cheek as she saw the labor of love that Charlie, the black smith, had put into this artisans work of art surrounding the cemetery.

The buggy circled the oak which was the anchor for the hammock where the small graveyard lay in awesome silence. Then, as the buggy drew up to the gate, Mary saw the hand forged and beaten from wrought iron, and welded by heat and hammer to complete the swinging gate. There was a circle and in the center was a Celtic cross. Around the circle the words "NOW IN THE HANDS OF GOD."

Mary broke down and sobbed, so Charlie thought he had really made a bad decision to make the fence without permission. However, Mary calmed his fears when she leaned over and kissed him on the cheek, and said, "Oh, thank you, Charlie. It is so beautiful and thoughtful. Now no one will ever doubt that anyone but a great man and his family are buried in this hallowed ground."

The first of the cattle began to near the cow pens at the stockyards, and it seemed as far as the eye could see were cows were coming down the trail to the pens. They filled the pens and spilled over into the pasture a half a mile away, kept for just a case as this.

The buyer was sitting astride the top rail of the fence and looking at the cattle when Jeremiah and Earl Ray rode up.

"You boys should have taken these cows to Tampa. They would bring about five dollars a head more than the Cuban trade," the buyer told them.

"We done hear'd what the price had fell through the floor there in the Tampa yards," Jeremiah responded.

"Well, that was before the country declared war on Spain," the man told them. He then added, "This will be the last we can buy and send to Cuba."

While they were talking, another man rode up and whispered something to the man on the fence. He climbed down, looked at Jeremiah and Earl Ray, and said. "I'll be back in an hour. In the meantime you all come on into the office and wait there for me. I shouldn't be too long."

In less than an hour, the man with an officer and two soldiers came into the office. The officer was a colonel, and he was introduced to

Jeremiah and Earl Ray since they were the owners of the twenty thousand head of cattle at the pens.

"Well. Gentlemen, we have some good news for you. The United States Government will pay you thirty-three dollars a head for all your cattle in these pens. If you can have another thousand head here in a week we will continue to pay that amount.

"Is that United States a gonna pay we'uns in gold lack the Cuban buyer done Colonel?" Jeremiah asked.

"No sir, the government will pay you in Yankee gold. It will be delivered to any bank you name in Central Florida," the colonel replied,

"How about them Yankee gold dollars be in delivered to the Bent Penny Ranch?" Earl Ray asked

"I'm sorry, Sir. The gold must be delivered to a bank with a vault," Answered the colonel. Then he asked, "Don't you all have an account with the Florida National Bank in Tampa?"

"Yessir. We is got a 'count to a bank here in Tamper, but hits got mor'n it kin hold now from last round up. Yessir hit do," Jeremiah drawled. Then he added, "So's I reckon the truth is we ain't."

"So sir, you see we'uns jist been taking hit to the ranch and hit sets in the safe thar at tha ranch till we needs some of hit, or we has a wagon agoin to Kissimmee," Earl Ray spoke up. "We gotta special wagon to haul hit in to the house."

"Well, I'm sorry gentlemen, but we must deal with the bank. And you must deal with us, too. So please get set up with the bank in Tampa and let us get on with this deal," the colonel ordered,

"Colonel, kin y'all give me an hour to git in touch with Davy over to Tamper. Then I kin tell you bout the bank thang." Jeremiah stated.

In a few hours Jeremiah came back to the colonel and showed him the wire he had received from Davy. It showed the bank account number and the follow-up telegram to the colonel from the bank and everything was in order.

When the papers were signed for the cattle, and the counts were authenticated, Jeremiah handed the colonel the rock bags with the exact amount of rocks that there were cattle. The colonel kept the bags of rocks as a souvenir from his first dealing with cracker cowboys from Florida.

'How much money in Yankee gold aire we gonna git?" Earl Ray asked the colonel.

"Six hundred sixty thousand dollars in Yankee gold. That will be a little over one ton of gold coins," the colonel answered.

Jeremiah and Earl Ray thought about this on their way back to the ranch. Then Earl Ray said, "Mebbe we'uns brang back a wagon load o'gold ever time we'uns go to Tamper till hits all   of hits to home with us I reckon."

Jeremiah laughed and then he and Earl Ray turned their horses toward home.

The End

Printed in the United States
by Baker & Taylor Publisher Services